Stan Barstow was born and still lives in the West Riding of Yorkshire. He is married and has a son and a daughter. After working in the engineering industry, mainly as a draughtsman, he became a full-time writer in 1962.

His first novel, *A Kind of Loving*, was published in 1960. Since then he has published three volumes of short stories and eight more novels, including *A Raging Calm, Joby, A Brother's Tale* and, most recently, *Just You Wait and See*. His work is read and studied widely in schools. He has been published in the United States and translated into nine European languages. The Open University has conferred on Stan Barstow an Honorary Degree of Master of Arts.

He has won The Royal Television Society Award for Writers on two occasions and The Writers' Guild and BAFTA Awards for his television dramatisations, notably, *Joby, A Raging Calm* and for Winifred Holtby's *South Riding*.

A Kind of Loving became a feature film (director John Schlesinger) and a ten-part televison serial. *A Brother's Tale* was also televised in three episodes.

Author photograph by Neil Barstow.

Also by Stan Barstow

A KIND OF LOVING
THE WATCHERS ON THE SHORE
THE RIGHT TRUE END
THE DESPERADOES
THE GLAD EYE and other stories
JOBY
A RAGING CALM

and published by Black Swan

B-MOVIE

Stan Barstow

BLACK SWAN

B-MOVIE

A BLACK SWAN BOOK   0 552   99321 2

Originally published in Great Britain by Michael Joseph Ltd.

PRINTING HISTORY

Michael Joseph edition published 1987
Black Swan edition published 1988

This book is set in 11/12pt Mallard

Black Swan Books are published by Transworld Publishers Ltd., 61-63 Uxbridge Road, Ealing, London W5 5SA, in Australia by Transworld Publishers (Australia) Pty. Ltd., 15-23 Helles Avenue, Moorebank, NSW 2170, and in New Zealand by Transworld Publishers (N.Z.) Ltd., Cnr. Moselle and Waipareira Avenues, Henderson, Auckland.

Made and printed in Great Britain by
The Guernsey Press Co. Ltd., Guernsey, Channel Islands.

Prologue

In those days people still went on holiday by train and bus. Spain was where the onions came from. Abroad was for the privileged few. People went to places like Scarborough and Bridlington, Great Yarmouth and Southend, Bournemouth and Llandudno, Morecambe and Blackpool. They still do, but then they went in their millions, and without the freedom of the motor car they needed lodgings.

They still hanged people in those days, too. They hanged Ruth Ellis who shot her lover dead outside a pub in Hampstead. They hanged Derek Bentley, who never shot anybody but happened to be caught on a robbery with a lad who did and then served a prison sentence because *he* was too young to hang, the law said. 'Give it to them, Chris,' Bentley was reported as shouting. The idiom of countless gangster movies: 'Fill the bastards full of lead.' What a pity the lad had not been to a school which would have trained his instinct to call instead, 'Surrender the pistol, Chris,' which was what his defence maintained he had meant. You can't be too careful with a weapon like language: it can go off and kill somebody. And it's best not even to think about poor sixpence-in-the-shilling Timothy Evans, who went to the gallows for killing his baby before it was found that a mass murderer called Christie had been living in the house all the time.

But it all added spice to the Sunday papers; brought more exciting exhibits to Madame Tussaud's Chamber of Horrors ('Five pounds for anyone who will spend the

night in here alone'); and inoculated the dark haunting
of the underside of human endeavour into the psyches of
small boys who put coins into slots to witness the clock-
work tableaux of execution by rope and guillotine in
countless penny arcades and amusement parlours by
the bracing briny.

Saturday

This woman from next door came round to look at this feller who'd got back from his holidays and passed away sudden.

'Well, Alice,' she sez when she's seen him laid out; 'it might sound a funny thing to say, but he does look well.'

'Look well?' the wife sez. 'Look well? He ought to look well; he's just had a fortnight at Blackpool.'

Chapter One

It is going to rain. That is sure. The only question is whether it will hold off long enough to let people get clear of the town. An August Saturday and the opening of Cressley's annual holidays; once a single week, now in the recent post-war years a fortnight – a sign, with the five-day week, of the enhanced status of the workers. All morning they have been pouring out to coast and countryside by every available means of transport, leaving behind factories, mills and warehouses silent and empty except for the creep of cats, the tread of watchmen's feet and the remote whistle and clank of maintenance men who, like entertainers, work while the rest of the world relaxes.

All morning, too, the storm clouds have been piling up to the south of the town, darkening the sky and bringing on early lights in the shops along the thoroughfares of the town centre. The air has become close, oppressive, and in the morning twilight of the gathering storm the smoke-soiled buildings seem to crowd in on one another; until now, towards noon, lightning cuts through the piled darkness of clouds and thunder cracks directly over- head. The first, heavy scattered drops of rain lay the dust in the streets; then within seconds a steady deluge is confining shopping stay-at-homes to the shelter of department stores and arcades, there to exchange knowing and resigned nods over the fact that this, after ten days of brilliant sunshine, should be the weather on the first day of the holidays.

Chapter Two

One man at least is glad of the rain as he moves, a solitary figure, hugging the walls along a glistening back street near the middle of town: a man in a mackintosh, his face hidden by the defensive crouch of his head and shoulders and the dripping low-pulled brim of a felt hat.

Nearby the rain is leaving brassy veins on the grimy spheres of a pawnbroker's sign over the door of a small shabby shop. It is the only shop left in a street awaiting demolition. Behind the old-fashioned small-paned window, odd bits of jewellery and various trinkets are scattered among household utensils and gadgets in a dusty confusion. The interior, set down two steps below the street, is in almost perpetual semi-darkness, overshadowed as it is by the towering façade of a gloomily empty chapel across the cobblestones. An adjustable lamp of dingy brass on the counter of the shop sheds a pool of light, deepening the shadows round the old man working there. A battered blue-painted alarm-clock by the old man's elbow shows a few minutes before twelve-thirty. He is counting the contents of his till before closing for lunch, while his middle-aged niece, her raincoat on and her shopping-bag in her hand, stands at the window, looking out.

'. . . ninety-two, ninety-three, ninety-four, ninety-five . . . and five new ones straight out of somebody's wage packet, makes a hundred.'

The old man catches his breath with an asthmatic wheeze and takes more loose notes.

'Don't you want the big light on?' his niece asks.

'No, I can see well enough. You get off for your dinner. I just want to check this money and get it into the safe before lunchtime.'

'You'll have a quiet time of it the next fortnight.'

'A famine before and after a feast. They've redeemed their best clothes and suitcases and left me their clocks and cutlery till they come back.' He chuckles.

'It surprises me that pawnbroking pays at all these days, when everybody that wants it is in work.'

'I suppose there'll always be the improvident to cater for. I make a living, what with this and that.' 'That' was lending money at exorbitant rates of interest.

'Aye, and you always will, you crafty old man.'

'Tchk, tchk. What a way to speak to your old uncle.'

'I know. Anyway, look, it's not going to 'bate, so I'll have to run through it.' She opens the door, setting the bell jangling. 'D'you want me to drop the latch?'

'No, no. It's still a few minutes off closing time. Who knows what orphan of the storm might be blown in yet?'

With a word about bringing back his weekend shopping that afternoon, she is gone.

The man approaching steps into the cover of a ginnel as he sees her come out of the shop and stand for a moment fiddling with the catch of her umbrella. He waits to see which way she will go. As she begins to walk away from him he crosses the street and continues along the pavement behind her. She has turned the corner before he reaches the shop.

When the door opens, setting the bell going again, the old man peers over his half-lenses into the shadows. It is as a sharper sound, like the snap of the Yale lock, follows the closing of the door that he feels a first faint touch of unease and glances down at the banknotes on the counter before him; all this in the few seconds before the man steps into view. Water drips from the sodden brim of his hat. The old man thinks that the handkerchief is to wipe his visitor's face but realises his mistake as the stranger's other hand comes into sight, the Service revolver with a shortened barrel held in it.

11

'Who are you? What do you want?'

'That.' The gun moves, indicating the money.

'Is this some kind of game?' The old man is sweeping the banknotes towards him. 'You can't just walk in and take what you want.'

'Back away,' the man tells him. 'Turn and face the wall and there'll be no trouble.'

But the old man cannot take his eyes off him. 'Who are you?' His eyes narrow. 'Don't I know you?'

'Back up,' the man orders. 'Do as you're told.'

He motions with the gun. With the old man turned away he can pick up the cash. It has never occurred to him that the old man might, as he does now, make a sudden dash for the rear premises. It startles him. He lifts the gun and strikes. The old man goes down, his fall pushing wide the partly open door he was running for.

The man looks down at him for perhaps five seconds and curses. Then he has himself in hand again as he scoops banknotes off the counter and pushes them deep into his raincoat pockets. He slips the gun into his pocket also and switches off the lamp. At the door he turns the card that hangs behind the glass and pulls down the blind. He looks quickly both ways along the street before stepping out and pulling the door shut behind him. The lock snaps home. He glances down at the card, which says 'CLOSED', and walks quickly away.

The rain has almost stopped. At the corner the man slows his pace before strolling on to the main thoroughfare, where he is soon lost to view in the crowds now returning to the streets.

Chapter Three

When Arny came back he was carrying the soaked trousers he had changed out of in the train toilet. The thin, fair young man sitting in the window corner watched him as he slung his case back up on to the rack and arranged the wet trousers so that they hung to dry, answering Arny's grin with a smile of affection that transformed, like a light from inside, the habitual serious cast of his face. For the present they had the compartment to themselves.

'How'd you manage to get so thoroughly drenched?'

'How'd you manage to keep so dry?' Arny countered. 'You must have been on the station hours if you missed the storm.'

'I thought you were going to miss the train.'

'Oh, I'd one or two things to see to. And my mother would hang on to me till the last minute.'

'Were you late getting up from London last night?'

'Yes. I couldn't get away till early evening. "You come home for the first time in months, use the place like a boarding house for one night, then take your hook to the seaside." '

'Is that what she said?'

' "Why can't you spend a few days with your parents, instead of rushing off with Frank? We don't see hide nor hair of him either, you know; and he's not two hundred miles away." '

'I didn't know she missed me.'

'She doesn't miss you, Frank. She begrudges you not missing her. You ought to keep going round and

13

telling her how grateful you are for all she did for you.'

'I did,' Frank said quietly.

'Rubbish.'

'I did, though,' Frank insisted.

'Crap. The old lady gets worse. She just can't get it through her head that I'm a big boy now. She spends sleepless nights with visions of what might happen to me in wicked London. Every time I walk in – which is once in a blue moon nowadays, I admit – she starts with her questions. Does my landlady treat me right? Have I got a girl friend? Do I wear my thick vests in winter? You can laugh, but she does. It's pathetic. She asked me this morning if I went to church. I don't know why, because there's nobody going to heaven but her. Give the old man his due, he never was a hypocrite. He sends his regards, by the way.'

'It's your dad I get the conscience about, really,' Frank said. 'You know your mother and I didn't hit it off that last bit when you'd gone into the army and I was still waiting for my call-up. Your dad was always pretty decent, though.'

'Decent he might be, but he's given in to her all their married life. What they did for you was no more than anybody else would have done in the same circumstances. They couldn't turn their backs on their own kith and kin. I'm surprised you didn't leave Cressley after your National Service, like I did. What's this town ever done for you, I'd like to know?'

'Oh, you feel obligations, ties . . .'

'Sod obligations, bugger ties.' Arny flung himself down in the opposite seat and offered cigarettes. They lit up. 'Anyway, forget them and all that. It's years since we had more than a few hours together. Now we've got a week. The old firm, eh?'

With the light dancing in his eyes, as of old, Arny began to sing a song they had once known, a song with a bawdy lyric that really went best after a few drinks:

If you should see our Sarah Jane
Swinging her fat arse down the lane . . .

Another line or two had Frank laughing as the carefree adolescent obscenity of the verses took him back over the lonely years to the jokes and adventures of their shared boyhood.

As Arny finished he slapped his knee and said, 'Remember the time I was singing that in the chapel vestry and the parson walked in? What was it he said? I don't just remember.'

'He said it was a good tune and asked if it was a Salvation Army hymn.'

'A Salvation Army hymn! That's right!'

They were running into a station. There looked to be too many people on the platform for them to keep their privacy and Arny got up and folded the hanging trousers and laid them on top of his case.

'I wonder if it'll be a good week for crumpet,' he said. 'God, I must tell you about a piece I met the other week. In a club in Stepney, it was. I was down there flogging the old one-armed bandits when she— What's up? Somebody you know?'

Frank, obviously not listening, had half-lifted himself out of his seat as he craned to look at something outside. But it didn't belong to her, the dark head that bobbed through the crush and was lost to view in the entrance to the subway. He had known it wasn't her, while the mere possibility of its being so was setting his pulse racing; which perturbed him still more, because it meant that she was still in his system, though it was months since she had sat in the car with the tears streaming down her face and told him what she was going to do.

He slumped back into his corner as the door slid open and people crowded in. With Arny here it was easier to see everything in a more reasonable light. Arny cut things down to their proper size. He had loved a girl whom he had thought loved him, and lost her because she didn't love him enough. An old story, and so what?

Arny would say. So she wasn't worth the heartache. Be thankful you found out when you did and not later. There are millions of girls in the world. Find another one and have fun. 'Lock up your daughters, the Whitmores are here!' The old phrase drummed in Frank's mind to the rhythm of the wheels. He smiled to himself, looking at Arny's familiar face and the misleading innocence of his blue eyes. They were together again and it was just like old times. They were together again and in for a wonderful week.

Chapter Four

The loco expelled steam with a savage hiss as they moved with the throng down the platform to the barrier, and as its odour filled Frank's nostrils he was suddenly irresistibly drenched in the magic of childhood holidays: the few fragmentarily vivid occasions with his father and mother and, more recent, those wartime weeks by the sea with Uncle Vernon and Aunt Carrie and, of course, Arny. From the booking-hall they could see the tumult of traffic in the narrow street and when they had made their way out on to the pavement by the row of taxis with their orange-fluted bonnets they stopped and looked up together, their gaze drawn beyond the cream face of the Woolworth building, to follow the criss-cross pattern of steel as the Tower soared above them into a rain-grey sky. Then Arny seemed to endorse the unexpected tightening of Frank's heart when he turned with a quick smile that surely came straight from the lad he had once been inseparable from, and said, 'Here we are, then! Good old Blackpool!'

As the trains disgorged the travellers to stand and gape or otherwise hesitate on the pavement outside the station, the men in cloth caps and mufflers pressed their advantage: 'Carry your case, sir? Carry your case, missis?' On occasion they would meet with success and stow under their arms an amazing weight and bulk of luggage to be carted off briskly into the crowds, hotly pursued by suddenly anxious holiday-makers fearful of letting them out of their sight.

Arny brushed aside their offers and led the way to a

taxi. Frank took a letter from his pocket and read out an address. 'Hope it's all right,' he said. 'I picked it at random.'

'It'll be okay,' Arny said easily. 'As long as we have comfortable beds and decent grub—' They were jerked forward as the driver braked to let a chauffeur-driven Bentley get by. Arny's head turned to watch it. 'One thing for sure – that character isn't paying fifteen bob a day at a crummy boarding house. The Imperial for him.' He sat back as the taxi nosed into the traffic. 'Maybe we can call in the bar one evening and have a drink.'

'The Imperial?' Frank knew where it was and what it looked like but had never thought of going in.

'Why not? They don't bite poor people like us as long as we behave ourselves.' He grinned. 'Piano players go in through the tradesmen's entrance.'

Chapter Five

The house was typical of its kind and identical with all the others in the street. It had a red-brick front and stood three storeys above ground level. Angular bay windows overlooked the street from the first two floors and a dormer window in the roof indicated an attic room. Five wide stone steps led up to the front door, which was set back in a porch. To the left of these a narrower and steeper flight of steps led down to a basement entrance.

Arny pressed the bell again. Through the open door they could see along the narrow hall. There looked to be two rooms on the left. A flight of stairs led up on the right. Near the door stood a hall-stand with a mirror. Across from it hung a barometer with its hand hovering between 'change' and 'fair' and a green baize notice-board with tapes holding business cards and leaflets advertising attractions and entertainments.

From somewhere in the basement a woman's voice called 'Brenda!' There was no reply that they could hear and in a few moments a woman appeared through a doorway under the stairs and hurried towards them, wiping her hands on her apron. She was small and slightly built, with an arid, faded look, as though all the nature had been dried out of her. Her black hair, scraped back into a bun, had a dusting of grey about her ears. Her harassed expression fitted exactly into the deep lines of her face as she peered shortsightedly at Frank and Arny, who had stepped in over the threshold.

Frank was holding his letter. 'Mrs Truscott?'

'What name is it?'

'Whitmore.'

'Whitmore . . . Two of you. Two young men . . .' She found a slip of paper on the hall-stand. 'My niece Brenda usually receives our guests but I don't know where she's got to.' She thrust the piece of paper at Frank. 'I can't read this without my glasses. Does it say room nine?'

'Yes, nine.'

'I'll show you up. You've got nice time to freshen up before tea.' She turned at the bottom step. 'You did expect to share a room?'

'Oh, yes. That's all right.'

'We have very few singles. They don't pay. If people want singles I tell them they'll have to go to a hotel.' She pointed along a dim corridor at the first landing. 'Bathroom and toilet.' She led them up another flight at the same brisk pace and waited for them to catch up. 'I guessed you were young people; that's why I put you up here. I put the older people lower down.' She opened a door. 'I think you'll find it comfortable.'

Arny pointed to a further flight of steps leading into the top of the house. 'Does anybody sleep up there?'

'Only my niece, Brenda.'

'It's to be hoped *she* doesn't keep forgetting her glasses.'

Mrs Truscott gave him a quick glance but said nothing. She was about to turn away when she told them, 'Oh, by the way, the front door's locked at half-past eleven. If you're going to be out after that, see Brenda for a key.' She went.

The room was small and simply furnished with two single beds, a wardrobe, a square dressing-table and a straight-backed chair by the window, all in a cheap light wood from which most of the polish had long since been scratched, blistered by sun or eaten away by the salt air. A skimpy carpet with an indeterminate pattern lay over the lino. Frank went to the window and looked out. Directly opposite were the backs of the houses in the next street and the area between was fenced off into yards. Through a gap in the line of houses he could see floating the ornate steel platforms of the top of the Tower.

'Well,' he said as he turned.

'Well what?'

'Not up to much, is it?'

'There's nothing here we haven't seen before, Frank. We can put up with it for a week. Pity there's no wash-basin, though. That means fighting for the bathroom. Which bed do you want?'

'I'm easy.'

'I'll take this one, then.'

Arny sat on the edge of the bed nearest the door then swung up his legs to stretch out. The mattress creaked. He laughed and bounced a little, then lay silent for a time as Frank emptied his case.

'Yes,' Arny said after a time, 'we must have a look in at the Imperial. I like to see where the brass hangs out and how them that have it behave themselves. I've had drinks and observant little half-hours in all kinds of places in London: the Savoy, the Ritz, Claridges . . .'

'Do you remember what Ernest Hemingway said to Scott Fitzgerald?'

'I'm ashamed to tell you I don't think I ever knew.'

'Well, Fitzgerald said, "The rich are different from you and me," and Hemingway said, "Yes, they have more money." '

'Dead bloody right,' Arny said. 'Take me. I was born to be rich. I don't mean titled or upper-crust, I mean loaded. But it looks as though I'm going to have to do it all for myself.'

'How do you propose to do it?'

'Oh, there are ways . . . What's your ambition?'

'It's not to make money for its own sake.'

'There's no such thing as money for its own sake, Frank. Money gives you choice. It gives you power. It lets you tell people to piss off. You're always on about the kind of music you want to play—'

'Am I?'

21

'You've told me. You know what I mean. If you had the dough you could form your own band; play at a loss if necessary, but play what you wanted. And if you'd had fifteen thou in the bank you wouldn't be pining for that Doris.'

'Who says I'm pining?'

'Admit it, Frank. Own up. You were real gone on that one and the bitch went after the money.'

'Just as well I found out what her priorities were.'

'You want to be loved for your own sweet self, is that it? Poor but honest.'

'Don't you?'

'There's more to a man than the colour of his eyes or whether his hair curls,' Arny said. 'Or even the length of his prick. A bird likes to see he's got something about him: that he's the boss, knows what he's doing, where he's going. She likes to know that he won't let anybody stand in his way. Then she can relax and feel safe herself.'

The bed creaked again as he moved. He lay on his back, his hands linked under his head. He had closed his eyes and was silent now for so long Frank thought he had fallen asleep. But at the sound of the gong being beaten in the hall below he immediately lifted himself on one elbow.

'I was hoping to have a wash before eating,' Frank said.

'Better be quick or your lettuce'll go cold.' Arny got up, put his jacket back on and crouched before the dressing-table glass to run a comb through his thick dark hair. 'A few leaves of lettuce,' he said, 'a tomato, a hard-boiled egg, a slice or two of cucumber, a few rings of raw onion (think who you might be face to face with tonight before you gobble them down), maybe a radish—'

'And a couple of slices of boiled ham,' Frank said.

'And a couple of slices of boiled ham.'

Chapter Six

They were wrong about the boiled ham. Tongue was on the plates. 'Bloody posh, man,' Arny muttered as they stood in the doorway of the dining-room, wondering which was their table. They made their way to one in the corner which was still unoccupied and found on it a marker with their room number.

While waiting to be served they took in their fellow boarders. There were some middle-aged couples, two with teenage children, and a younger couple with a girl of about five. The only guests of their own age seemed to be two very plain and retiring young women who sat near the door and kept their eyes down, as though waiting for the years to pass quietly and transform them into replacements for the elderly spinsters sharing a table in the window bay with a distinguished-looking old man and his frail wife. The youngish man with the small girl had a hard, metallic humourless laugh, more a nervous reflex than a sign of amusement. One of the middle-aged men, thick-set, red-faced, with a round close-cropped skull and a jacket of violent hairy tweed – the colour, Arny pointed out later, of diarrhoea – had pinned down the couple sharing his table and was delivering a monologue which informed them and most of the rest of the room of how many years he had been visiting Blackpool, that it was not the same place since the war, that during the war it had been over-run and plagued by those 'damned Yanks' and that there was nothing anybody could tell him about the town, its surroundings or its history. His victims, a small bespectacled man and his matching wife, looked like the last people to presume to tell anyone anything; but the loud man had issued what amounted to a challenge and was going on to substantiate his claim in a voice which cut like a buzz-saw through the hum of general conversation. His wife, who had presumably endured the histrionics of this know-all for some years, kept silent except for an occasional nod or a 'yes' when, for the sake of further emphasis, she was called upon to confirm her husband's statements. The loud man's chairback was almost touching the closed lid of an upright piano.

'Well, they've packed 'em into here,' Arny said, 'but where the hell do they fit 'em all in upstairs?'

As he spoke his attention was drawn to something else and a signal with his eyes took Frank's head round. The woman who had brushed past them in the doorway had come in again with a loaded tray.

' "My niece Brenda" I assume,' Arny said.

Frank was to imagine later a slight resemblance to Mrs Truscott in the girl's face, but there any likeness ended. For everything that in the older woman was dried and faded was in the younger ripe and ample, yet tautly under control. The heels of her platform-soled grey suede shoes made her taller than her medium height. Over a tight black skirt she wore a short frilled apron which somehow suggested that her commitment to domestic service was no more than part-time, her true vocation lying elsewhere. Her jaw was too heavy for prettiness and her skin was pitted in places, but she charged the atmosphere of the room with a sexual energy that everyone must have been aware of and which openly delighted Arny. Her hair had had what Frank had once heard a friend of Arny's mother's call 'the benefit of the bottle' and the girl brushed a strand of it back off her face as she came to them and rested her tray on their table, freeing one hand and bringing to a level with Arny's appreciative gaze the high, pointed breasts held in the fine clinging wool of her green sweater.

24

'You found your table, then.' She put a plate of salad in front of each of them.

'We put two and two together,' Arny said. 'You must be Brenda.'

'That's me.'

'I knew from your auntie's description: "a good-looking fair girl with a marvellous figure".'

'Crikey,' Brenda said, 'you're quick out of the trap, aren't you?'

'Have to be. Time's against us.'

'It's against me, that I do know,' Brenda said. 'I'll go and fetch your tea-pot.'

She left them, Arny leaning over to catch a glimpse of her legs through gaps between the chairs. She had pigeon toes and was very slightly bow-legged. Arny drew in his breath.

'Jeeze. I really go for just-apart knees. Don't know why, but they get me going.'

'She's taken your number, mate,' Frank said. He unscrewed the cap of the salad-cream bottle and sniffed at the contents before putting some on the edge of his plate.

'It's not to say she doesn't like it,' Arny said.

She came back, bringing them a pot of tea and a jug of hot water.

'Do your duties leave you free to go on the town Saturday night?' Arny asked.

It was either too twisted a sentence for her or she felt she had to play for time.

'Beg pardon.'

'Do you get Saturday night off?'

'I get what I want off.'

'Lucky you. Why I ask, though, is that your auntie said to see you if we wanted a late key and it struck me that if you'd nothing better to do you might consider showing a few of the sights to a couple of strangers to the town.'

'Down, Rover,' Brenda said. 'Eat your lettuce and cucumber. It'll cool your blood.'

Chapter Seven

Frank was down again first, washed and tidied for the evening. Everybody seemed to have gone out. He wandered into the empty dining-room, moved a chair and opened the piano. His fingers found the chords of 'Someone to Watch Over Me' and he blocked its outlines very slowly and out of tempo, resisting the spaces between the phrases that his speed offered for decorative runs. The piano wasn't up to that kind of fancy stuff.

Brenda came in. 'Oh, it's you.' Is it? he wondered. 'I couldn't think who might be playing.' She took a little brass-plated crumb pan and brush and began to sweep the tablecloths and tidy the cruets and sauce bottles. 'Do you play for money?'

'Try me.'

He realised that he wasn't scared of her; because he didn't want her. He conceded that she might strip splendidly. But morning always came.

'I mean is it your living?'

'It has been from time to time.'

'You can always tell the real professional touch. We get a lot of bangers. They're all right in a sing-song.'

Frank slipped into an easy mid-tempo rendition of 'I do Like to be Beside the Seaside' and Brenda said over it, 'That's better. You shouldn't be feeling miserable at the beginning of your holidays.'

'Pensive,' Frank said.

'If I knew what it meant I might agree with you.'

Arny appeared and stood in the doorway. 'Ah so!'

Frank finished with a flourish and shut the lid.

Arny seemed quite happy to contemplate the curves of Brenda's hips and behind as she bent over the tables. She glanced round.

'Haven't you any hidden talents, then?'

'I'll be happy to demonstrate them,' Arny said, 'at a more suitable time and place. Say later tonight, venue your choice?'

'Don't refuse any good offers on the strength of it,' she told him.

Chapter Eight

The two young men came through the back streets from the house and on to the Promenade by Central Pier. There was no rain but it had turned very cold. The sea, at high tide, hurled spray as it recoiled from its heavy lurch against the Promenade wall and the breeze it had brought searched every opening in their clothing.

They walked north at a steady pace. Behind them the Promenade with its carriage-way, its tramtracks and its wide pavements curved out of sight by Central Pier; before them it ran straight as far as the granite needle of the War Memorial. In the hinterland behind this central section of promenade, the Golden Mile, lay the heaviest concentration of the town's amusements: cinemas, theatres, ballrooms; the West-End-style extravaganzas of the Winter Gardens and the Opera House; and the shabby near-nude peepshows of the Promenade itself. And over all, giving majestic focus to the theatres and cinemas, the Pleasure Beach to the south, the parks and the three piers, dominating all the town and the country-side for miles inland, was the Tower: that colossal upraised finger of steel, beckoning to their Mecca seven million pleasure-seeking pilgrims a year, drawing them into the pulsing mass, the brash vitality of its rowdy life, the human sea which surged and eddied in innumerable cross-currents, the dull rumble of traffic sounding the undersurge and the mournful warning hoot of trams the cry of the gulls.

Arny responded to it all with eyes that glinted with impudent challenge. When two lasses on the spree came screaming down the pavement towards them they caught Arny's grin and checked as they drew level, leaning on each other as their laughter subsided into speculation, then tossing their heads in a pantomime of disdain and calling after the two young men as they walked on without stopping.

'Willing,' Arny said, 'but too noisy. No refinement.'

'Where are we going?' Frank asked, though he was quite happy to keep on walking for a while. 'Have you anything in mind?'

'Well,' Arny began, smiling, 'when I got the key from Brenda she just happened to mention that she'd be dancing at the Tower Ballroom tonight.'

'That suits me,' Frank said. 'I intended looking up Johnny Longden before the week was out, and it may as well be tonight.'

'Longden?'

'I don't think you'd know him. He's playing in the Tower band.'

At North Pier Arny said, 'Well, a breath of sea air's all right in moderation, but I'm perished. Let's go in for a jar.'

They crossed the road, dodging traffic, in the direction of Talbot Square. Here the crowds clogged the pavements and until they got away from the Front it was impossible to walk together. Frank finally caught Arny up as he waited by the open door of a pub. They went in, to find packed rooms and hardly a space in which to stand.

'We'll have one, seeing as we're in,' Arny said, 'then shove off somewhere else.'

He edged his way into the throng lining the bar counter and came back – much sooner, Frank thought, than he would have done – carrying two halves of bitter and two measures of whisky.

'Who's all the Scotch for?'

' "Who's all the Scotch for?" Arny mimicked. 'Get one of 'em down you and make your happy soul miserable.'

He steered Frank into a suddenly vacated space by a

radiator on whose shelf he rested his drinks while he began to search his pockets.

'I had to copper up to pay,' he said, 'I can't find my wallet.'

'Sure you had it when you came out?'

'Positive.' He had examined every pocket in turn. 'No, it's gone. I must have lost it between here and the digs.' He was silent for a moment. Then he said decisively, 'I've had me pocket picked, old lad. That crowd in Talbot Square: a pickpocket's delight.'

'Let's go and report it to a copper.'

'A fat lot of good that'd do. They wouldn't know where to start looking. Whoever's got it will have ditched the evidence by now: the wallet in a waste-bin, the cash in his own pocket.' He swallowed half his Scotch and followed it with a mouthful of beer. 'Well, I can say good-bye to that. A good job I wasn't carrying all my holiday money, that's all.'

'How much?' Frank asked.

'Oh, three or four quid. I'm not sure exactly.'

'It's enough. I think we should report it.'

'No point.'

'There's always a chance.'

'Forget it. I've seen the last of it. It's written off.'

Frank took three one-pound notes from his own note-case and pushed them into Arny's hand. 'Take this to see you through tonight.'

'Sure you're not leaving yourself short?'

'Sure.'

'Thanks, then. I shall need it. Getting Brenda round to my way of thinking mightn't be difficult, but it'll be to pay for.'

Chapter Nine

Round and round the huge dance-floor of the Tower Ballroom a jostling horde of young people on holiday circled to the brassy urgings of a quickstep. Almost as many more looked on from the perimeter seats. It needed all the firmness of the corps of green-uniformed attendants to keep the dancers moving in one vast orderly circle, as the music drove on, belting out over their heads to the galleries of spectators' seats and rising to the lofty plaster carvings of the ceiling under which, at intervals, moulded cartouches bore the names of the great composers: Beethoven, Mozart, Handel, Brahms . . .

Arny said, 'Hell's bells! How do you find anybody in this lot?'

As a set ended the attendants ushered everyone off the floor to pack the seats and the walks under the galleries. Frank and Arny pushed farther into the hall and a tall youth with prominent eyes, a d. a. haircut and a long, velvet-collared jacket spun on them as they squeezed by.

'Who d'ye think you're pushing?'

He was looking for trouble. Arny turned on him and smiled ingratiatingly. 'Sorry, mate. No damage done, I hope.' He had his hand out and took the youth's into it while the lad was deciding how to deal with someone who backed down so fast. Frank, watching the boy's face, saw something change in his eyes. Arny, still holding him in the apparent attitude of shake and make up, leaned in and spoke into his ear. The lad looked down stupidly at his hand as Arny released it and withdrew, moving away from the encounter now without a backward look.

'Teds,' Arny said when he and Frank had finally found a place where they could stand together and watch the floor. 'Not so many of 'em up here yet, but London's crawling with 'em. They're not all as stroppy as that one.'

'What did you do to him?'

'I told him he'd only to say the word and I'd put him on his knees. I had my thumb on a nerve. I could have bent him double.' He smiled at Frank. 'What did *you* learn in the forces?'

It was Frank who saw Brenda first as, some time later, she came by, on the dance-floor, in the arms of a stocky man with sidewhiskers and a home-and-dry smile.

'There she is.'

Arny nodded as he spotted her too. 'Keep an eye out for her coming round again. Bushy there looks as if he thinks it's sealed and delivered and only to sign for. Time I put my claim in.' He handed Frank a Yale key. 'You'd best have this, then if we get split up you can get into the house. Brenda will have her own.' He took hold of Frank's arm. 'Listen, will you be okay by yourself if I make progress?'

'Sure. Enjoy yourself.'

'Pick one out for yourself and get going.'

'I'll see. Here she comes again.'

'Don't wait up for me.'

Arny walked out on to the floor, twisting between the dancing couples, and tapped Brenda's partner on the shoulder. He turned his head, glowering, but Arny, smiling at Brenda, walked round the other side of him and, forcing Brenda to lengthen her stride, guided her away across the floor. The sidewhiskered youth came and stood next to Frank. He couldn't quite believe the smoothness with which he had been made to relinquish his prey.

'D'ye see that?' he asked.

'I did.'

'Fuckin' cheek.'

'Making headway, were you?'

'I fuckin' was.'

'He's an old boy friend of hers, just back from abroad.'

'How d'you fuckin' know?'

'I know them both.'

'You won't be on my fuckin' side then, will you?'

'I'm neutral.'

'Oh, aye.'

Muttering something about getting 'a fuckin' drink' the lad moved off and Frank lit a cigarette and wondered if he would do the same. But he didn't drink much, and hardly ever alone. Nor did he really want to dance. Those girls not already on the floor who were not with men were in couples or small groups. He would have to choose one whose face and figure he liked (or didn't dislike), even though he would probably never see her again, and run the risk of her not liking the look of him. Then he might pick someone to whom dancing was more than just a social pleasure or an excuse to get your hands on a presentable member of the opposite sex; and he was sadly out of practice (in both activities, come to that), most of his time in dance-halls having been spent on the stand rather than on the floor. His mind rehearsed the words that would pass for conversation; about the quality of the band, the floor, how hot and how crowded it was, what part of the country she was from, did she specially like Blackpool, did she prefer the Tower to the Winter Gardens, did she come every year, why wasn't she with her boy friend, don't say a good-looking girl like her wasn't spoken for.

He made his way nearer to the bandstand until he could pick out Johnny Longden.

Chapter Ten

'Well how are you, then, whack?' Longden asked, grinning broadly as he pumped Frank's hand. It was the interval. The band had left the stand for a breather. 'What are you doing here?'

'I'm with all these other people.'

'Playing the punter for a change, eh?' Longden turned to the slim dark-haired girl to whom he'd been talking when Frank came up. 'Do you two know each other? Rona Fairlie, Frank Whitmore.'

There was a shyness in her eyes; even, Frank could imagine, a faint colour come new to her cheeks, as she offered a fine-boned hand.

'I know him but he doesn't know me.'

'How's that?' Frank asked.

'God! what it must be like to be famous,' Johnny Longden said. He took each of them by the arm. 'Let's go and get a drink. I've blown myself dry.'

Longden, like Arny, was quicker back from the busy bar than Frank thought he would have been himself; though probably the band uniform gave priority. He handed Rona a gin and tonic, Frank a half of beer and took the top off his own pint with an appreciative gasp.

'Ah! That's better.' He wiped froth from the heavy moustache which partly covered his mouth and asked Frank, 'How do we sound from the floor?'

Frank hesitated and Longden said, 'It's like that, is it?'

'You all sound a bit bored.'

'Never expect this man to flannel about music, Rona,' Longden said to the girl. 'He doesn't know how.' He sighed. 'Some nights we rise to the mediocre but mostly we're crap.'

'Now you're taking it right over the top,' Frank said. 'You're a well-tuned, well-balanced outfit doing what you're called on to do with professional ease.'

'But we sound a bit bored.'

'And your ensemble's slack.'

'I thought you'd never mention that.'

'You need a rehearsal to put the cutting edge back,' Frank said.

'And wouldn't it be wonderful if we had our very own book to give us our very own style, while we're about it?'

'I could sell you one.'

'I know, mate, I know. But we run-of-the-mill pros have to live in the world as it is, not as we'd like it to be.'

'Which is one reason I'm not joining,' Frank said.

'Are you still pounding it at the Gala Rooms?'

'No, I left months ago.'

'A better offer?'

'A difference of opinion with Kane.'

'I see. I heard he'd got married again.'

'He married Doris Preston.'

'The piece who sang with the band?' As Frank nodded Longden glanced at Rona. So he knew something as well. 'You are still playing, though, aren't you? Or are you totally absorbed in writing arrangements for the bottom drawer?'

'I'm open to offers,' Frank said. 'I get in a couple of nights a week, here and there.'

'I ask you, Rona,' Longden said, 'to observe this gifted young man. He's got more music in his little toe than I have in my entire overweight body and he tots up figures by day and plays the piano two nights a week – when he's lucky.'

'Don't listen to him,' Frank said.

'No, don't listen to me. I'm just a poor bloody saxophone player. But Rona's heard you herself. Haven't you, Rona?'

'Oh, yes, many a time,' the girl said, the colour once

35

more in her cheeks. 'And he was certainly wasting himself where I heard him.'

'There you are, mate. Take it from a lady of discernment.' Longden glanced at his watch. 'I could murder another pint but I must go and pursue my humble livelihood. You talk to the lad, Rona. We must get together during the day, Frank.'

'Yes. I'll see you again, Johnny.'

He went. Frank, for what suddenly seemed like the first time, looked directly at the girl.

'We've got time for another drink, haven't we?'

'If you like. Thank you.'

Frank looked behind him. The crush had eased and a table come vacant. 'Sit down there. I'll be right back. I'm not keeping you, am I?' She looked puzzled. 'From something else? From someone else?'

'No.'

'So you live in Cressley, then?' he asked when he came back.'

'Just outside. Netherford.'

'And we had to come to Blackpool to meet.'

'Oh, I'm sure that happens every week.'

'All the same, I can't think why I never saw you at the Gala Rooms.'

'No. It's not very flattering.'

'You haven't dyed your hair. Had it cut differently . . .?'

'Shaved off my moustache, thrown away my dark glasses . . .?'

'Tell you the truth, from where I sat you hardly noticed anybody.'

'Keep working at it. You'll get there.'

'Trumpet players, sitting facing the floor, resting now and then – they've been known to see people.'

'In *Orchestra Wives* Cesar Romero saw everything from the piano?'

'*Orchestra Wives*?' Frank said. 'You're not old enough to remember *Orchestra Wives*.'

'If I'm not neither are you.'

36

'But I look out for the re-release of pictures like that. I've travelled miles to see them.'

'Well, I first saw it when I was about eight.'

'And fell for Cesar Romero.'

'Oh, no, I was mad about Tex Beneke.'

'Another saxophone-player.'

'Another?'

'Johnny, Tex Beneke.'

'Oh, Johnny. I've known Johnny since *before* I was eight.'

'What's the band like at the Gala Rooms nowadays?' Frank asked.

'Terrible.'

He laughed. 'Thanks.'

'When I didn't see you any more I took it for granted that you *had* gone on to better things.'

'Yes, well, you see, Johnny thinks I'm the best thing since Fletcher Henderson because he really hasn't got much music in him. He's a good reader and section man, quick, adaptable; but one set of notes is really much like another to him.'

'Who is Fletcher Henderson?'

'Do you know who Pete Rugulo and Ralph Burns are?'

'No. But I'll bet they aren't tennis-players.'

'We're getting warmer,' Frank said. 'What shall we eliminate next?'

'If you don't ask you never learn,' Rona said.

'True. And it's not everybody who's not afraid to acknowledge their ignorance.'

'Ignorance in the sense of not knowing, not uncouth?'

'Oh, quite. Who could ever call you uncouth?'

'Careful,' Rona said, 'there's a lot you don't know about me. In fact, almost everything.'

'Well, if you really want to know – and forgive me if you were only making polite conversation – Fletcher Henderson set the style for the pre-war Benny Goodman band. He was a pianist, but his niche in the Hall of Fame is as an arranger. Closer to us, Pete Rugulo wrote for Stan Kenton and Ralph Burns arranged for the post-war

Woody Herman band – The Third Herd. Then there's the great Eddie Sauter . . . But the sad truth, love, is that I'm ten years too late. The big bands are gone. Seven brass, five saxes, four rhythm, occasional vibes. In the bottom of my wardrobe there's the beginnings of a book for a band like that; a style that it looks as if nobody's ever going to hear.'

Looking up from his glass he saw Arny come into the room. One hand cupped Brenda's elbow. She wore a white blouse with a length of narrow black velvet ribbon tied in a bow at the neck. She stayed with Arny as he went to the bar and ordered. There was less of a crush there now. As he waited, Arny turned to face Brenda, one arm resting on the bar. He looked past her and saw Frank. Their eyes met, Arny raising his eyebrows and pulling down his mouth to signal that he was impressed with Rona. Frank gave him a little nod.

He said to Rona, 'Won't your friends be wondering where you are?'

'Won't yours?'

'I can see mine from here. He's quite happy with his present company.'

'So is mine,' Rona said. 'I was only a kind of decoy.'

'Snap!'

'But I couldn't say I was having an unprofitable evening. Not at all.'

'Me neither.'

She was telling him that she was enjoying his company. And that she obviously felt it necessary to come close to saying it outright unlocked in Frank a possibility of happiness that took him by surprise. He felt a broad grin form. He wanted his hands on her and hers on him.

'Would you like to go down and dance, then?'

'Yes, please.'

'I ought to warn you about my two left feet.'

'I don't believe you!'

'Wait and see.'

'Well, never mind,' Rona said, 'I can soon sort those out.'

'Can you?'

'Yes, of course I can.'

'It's the counting I can't seem to get the hang of,' Frank said.

They were standing. Rona took his arm.

'Come on,' she said, 'I never could resist a challenge.'

Chapter Eleven

She had taken his arm again, slipping hers through his quite naturally, soon after they left the Tower building and, turning away from the sea, set out to walk through the town. The tide was going out and it was warmer in the streets.

'I can easily get a taxi.'

'I'd *like* to take you,' Frank had said.

'In that case we could quite easily walk.'

Now, as they strolled unhurriedly through suburban avenues that could have been any town, he was talking to her without strain, as though, he reflected in one moment of mild surprise, she was someone he was accustomed to taking his bearings from.

But Rona stopped at a gate. 'Here we are.' The houses around them were small neat semis.

'Handy having relatives at the seaside.'

'I try hard not to abuse it.'

'Are they retired?'

'Well, Uncle Len's retired from the police force. He was a policeman here. Now he's a security officer for a store in town. But they're not as old as you mean. Will you come in and have some coffee? I know they'd like to meet you.'

'A bit late, isn't it?'

'Oh, they're night birds. They sit up till all hours.'

A door opened beyond the length of front garden. They heard the chink of milk bottles.

'Is that you, Rona?' the woman in the doorway called.

'Yes.'

'Have you got somebody with you?'

'A friend, from home.'

'Well, don't stand there, bring him in.'

She went back inside, leaving the door open.

'There you are,' Rona said; 'you can't get away now.'

Chapter Twelve

Sandwiches, biscuits with savoury spread and a home-baked fruit pie had appeared with the coffee, despite Frank's protest that he had just looked in to say hullo.

'If all you've had is a boarding-house tea at six o'clock, you'll be more than ready for another bite now,' Rona's aunt said.

She was in her fifties, her hair still mostly dark, her body pleasingly plump round small bones. Her husband was bigger, slack at the belly, long untidy strands of hair combed across to cover his bald head. He was washing his hands in the kitchen and now he appeared in the doorway with the towel.

'Been having a spot of bother over your way, I see.'

'Oh?'

Mrs Rogers said, 'Now, Len, I'm sure the young man isn't interested in crime.'

'Nonsense, Olive. Everybody's interested in crime. Or they should be. I only mentioned it because it happened on his doorstep.' He turned to get rid of the towel and came in rolling down his shirtsleeves.

'In Cressley?' Frank asked.

'What time did you travel?'

'The twelve forty-two train.'

'And you haven't seen an evening paper?'

'No.'

'Somebody robbed a pawnbroker's shop in Pym Street late on this morning. Cleared out the till and left the old man coshed and unconscious on the floor.'

'Pym Street?' Frank frowned. 'It's a demolition site. I

42

didn't know there were any shops left along there.'

'This villain did, seemingly. And he knew the best time to strike, so's he could get clear before the alarm was raised. The old chap usually closed for lunch, y'see.'

'So they haven't got anybody for it, then?'

'Not yet. But they will.'

'They will if they're lucky,' Rona's aunt put in. 'Whoever did it could be the other side of the country by now.'

'How could anybody from outside know about a set-up like that?' Rogers asked. 'It's a local job, and local lore is what will catch him. That and his own mistakes. The least little slip could grow into something big enough to nail him.'

'You know yourself how many they never catch, Len,' Rona's aunt said.

'All the same . . .' Rogers said.

'All the same,' Frank said lightly, 'I can't help feeling glad it's not me they're after.'

'As long as your conscience is clear,' Rogers said, without the slightest flicker of humour, 'you can rest easy.'

Rona caught Frank's eye. She winked and smiled. Again he felt happiness stir in him. He grinned in return.

'You can find your way back into town?' she asked him some time later, at the gate.

'Oh, I expect so.'

'Perhaps I'll walk you as far as the main road. It's easy from there.'

And perhaps, he thought, that would give him time to ask if he could see her again, as surely she wanted him to.

'We must be quite near Stanley Park here.'

'Less than ten minutes' walk.'

'I thought I might have a look in there tomorrow, if it's fine.'

'With your cousin?'

'With you, if you've nothing better to do.'

'Won't Arny mind?'

'Oh, he'll have other plans.'

'It's one of the rules, isn't it?'

'What?'

43

'If a lad clicks his pals leave him a clear field.'

'Have I clicked?'

'You've got a date, anyway.'

'Oh.'

'Could you call at the house for me, about half-past two?'

'If I can find it again.'

She laughed and told him the address, making him repeat it. They had reached the main road. She pointed across.

'See the church on the corner and the pub opposite? Take your bearings from them and if you get lost in the estate ask somebody. For now, you walk along here to the right until you come to the traffic lights. Turn left there and you'll be going directly back into town.' She held out her hand. 'I've had a lovely evening and I'll look forward to seeing you again tomorrow.' She turned and left him.

Her directness refreshed him. His tread was light as he walked away. He began to whistle. After a time shifting contrasts and blends of brass and reeds formed in his mind. He felt a rhythm and tempo unusual for that melody without being perversely 'different'. He liked it. It had possibilities. He would jot some of that down as soon as he had pen and paper.

Chapter Thirteen

There was a light in the basement and one in the hall, but nobody about downstairs as Frank let himself into the house. He took his toilet bag to the bathroom and washed his hands and face and brushed his teeth. Back in the room he undressed slowly, absent-mindedly, then got into bed and lay with the light on, waiting for Arny to come in. He had been thinking about Rona; but now, before he realised, he was thinking about Doris, going over it all again, going over what he had gone over so many times before. It was night-time and that had always been the time she could catch him unawares . . .

Chapter Fourteen

He had played the piano three nights a week at the Gala Rooms, leading the seven-piece band there, and the start of Doris had been one night when Kane called him into the office during the interval and after offering him a Scotch said,

'How do you think the customers would take to a canary, Frank?'

Kane could make Frank smile. At that time, he could. With his way of studding his speech with expressions lifted from Hollywood gangster films he often sounded like a not very good English actor trying to play American with a bad script. Women under a certain age were 'chicks'; people of low intelligence were 'lame brained'. Frank had heard someone being told to 'take a powder' and a girl singer had to be a canary.

'They'd love a good one; but where do you come across a good semi-pro?'

'I heard one the other night in a pub in Leeds. Just with piano and drums, but I was impressed enough to ask her to call in. She lives round here. Give her the once-over, Frank; tell me if she measures up.'

'Is she good-looking?'

'They'll look twice.'

'It is her voice I'm judging, though, isn't it?'

Kane didn't get it for a second and Frank could not have told him why he'd asked. Then: 'Voices you judge, Frank. Pussy, I audition myself.'

He wasn't, if it came to that, conspicuous for the number of women he took around. Though all his interests

46

were on the racier fringes of legitimate business – the Gala Rooms, a pub-restaurant, a couple of small cinemas, a bookmakers, shop property, a garage – he wasn't a conspicuous man. In his dapper daytime double-breasteds, and often a flower in his buttonhole, Kane kept his head down. Even the midnight-blue Rolls was as discreet as a car of that class could be in a town where few were seen regularly. And in a district where you could often trace a well-known man through various connections and perhaps back a generation or two, Kane was not to be pinned down. No one seemed to know quite where he had come from and why he had prospered in the West Riding. Even less was known about the ex-wife, once referred to in Frank's presence, but never seen.

With Doris it was the sound of her heels on the ballroom floor and the way she had walked out of the shadows into the light round the piano that Frank always recalled first. That and the wide blue of her stare, direct but apprehensive, like the look of a nervous child, so that he was on her side from the start. Her voice was husky and soft, with something of the timidity of her eyes in it, making him lean down from the stand to catch what she said.

'Is Mr Kane about, please? I'm Doris Preston. He asked me to call round.'

He gave her a chair and went to tell Kane. When he came back she was sitting just as he had left her, knees together, hands clasped in her lap.

He asked her what kind of songs she liked to sing.

'The old evergreens best, I think.'

'Ballads?'

'Mostly. But I can swing as well.'

'Do you model yourself on anybody in particular?'

'Oh, no!' She sounded genuinely horrified at the thought. 'I like Doris Day and Jo Stafford, and Lena Horne for the bluesy stuff; but I don't sing like them at all. You get nowhere being a broken-down imitation of somebody else.'

47

'Not even as a smooth and perfectly functioning imitation,' Frank said.

At which point Kane came out.

'Has Frank introduced himself? He leads the band here.'

'I guessed he was important.'

'Yes, he calls the shots in the music department, so I'm just going to sit at the back where you can forget about me. She's all yours, Frank.' And, indeed, for a time he had thought she was.

'Can you read?' he asked her.

'No, but I pick up a tune in no time.'

'Okay, let's find out where your voice lies. Sing me a few bars of something as you would if you were on your own.'

'Anything in particular?'

'Anything that comes to mind.'

' "I'm in the Mood for Love"?'

'Great. Start it and I'll pick you up.'

Thirty minutes later, when she had gone to the girls' room, Frank walked across to Kane.

'What do you think, Frank?'

'There's a lot of promise there.'

'Enough to take her on?'

'Enough for me.'

They both watched Doris as she came back down the side of the bandstand and, as though not aware that she was being observed, stood patiently waiting.

'That "little girl lost" manner of hers,' Frank said, 'could be a wow. Whether it's genuine or not.'

'Genuine or not doesn't matter,' Kane said. 'It's sexy. That matters.'

'Dor,' Kane suggested she call herself: 'Dor Preston'. And that was how she appeared on the posters outside and in the display ads in the papers: 'Frank Whitmore and the Gala Rooms Band. Resident Vocalist, Dor Preston.'

'Are you prepared to come in two or three nights and

rehearse with me, before you try with the band?' Frank asked her.

'Anything you say.' He felt the fascination growing in him as her eyes opened unbelievably wider. 'Does that mean you like me?'

'Oh, yes,' Frank said. 'We both like you.'

Chapter Fifteen

She couldn't read but she was a quick study, grasping the intricacies of a vocal line in a couple of run-throughs. Her natural ear delighted Frank. Her pitch was true and unfailing. She hit the note spot on and when she didn't you knew she had bent it from choice. He arranged some things especially for her and carved holes for her vocals in some of their stock arrangements. He felt fat with pride.

It seemed she could never tire of telling him, as she relaxed in his arms at the end of the street, where he halted the car, 'I love you, Frank. You're so good to me.'

She was still telling him that at the moment she told him that Kane had put in his bid.

'Marry? You're sure he said marry?'

He was ready to laugh with her at the absurdity of it until he realised that for her it was no laughing matter.

'What did you say?' He had not thought he would need to ask.

'I told him I loved you, Frank.'

'And what did he say to that?'

'He wouldn't listen. He said I'd soon forget you when I saw all the things he could do for me.'

He knew then that he had lost her, even though she began to cry, and he knew also that she was truly fond of him and truly torn between that and all that Kane could give her.

'Oh, Frank, I wish it had never happened. I'm so miserable.'

'There's a price to pay for everything,' he told her. 'At least you'll be miserable in comfort.'

She was surprised that he did not shout and swear, perhaps even that he did not strike her. But she had come to him without pressure and that was the way she must stay.

It had been only a few nights after that when he met Fred Nuttall. Frank was coming out of a pub, drunker than he could remember being since the RAF, when a hand emerged from the car-park shadows and clamped on to his arm.

'You're t'piano-player, aren't you?'

'What?'

'You don't know me but I know you. I've been watching you for over an hour. I'm Fred Nuttall an' you're the bugger what pinched my lass.'

'You've got the wrong bloke, mate,' Frank said. 'I don't know your girl.'

'Oh, but tha fuckin' does. Doris. "Dor" she calls herself now. Stupid fuckin' name, whoever thought it up. How is it you're suppin' on your own?' he wanted to know. 'Is she washin' her hair?'

'Doris,' Frank said, and began to laugh. 'You're behind with the news, mate. She's getting married, our Doris is.'

'When's she gettin' married?'

'I don't know. I shan't be going, though I wouldn't put it past their brass neck to invite me.'

Nuttall shook Frank. Frank's head felt loose on his shoulders.'

'Hang on,' he said, 'you're curdling the beer.'

'Who's she marryin'?'

'Larry Kane.'

'An' who's Mister Larry fuckin' Kane when he's at home?'

He still held Frank's arm in an unyielding grip.

Frank said, 'Look, I don't feel too cracky. Let's go and sit in the car.'

'If you want to throw up,' Nuttall said, 'get over in yon' corner. I'll dog out for you.'

'Good of you,' Frank said, 'but I'll be okay if I can sit down.'

He found his keys, unlocked the door, got in. Fred's bulk settled in beside him.

'Doris is engaged to marry Larry Kane, the owner of the Gala Rooms.'

'I thought she wa' thick wi' you.'

'She was. She was. Yes, I can't deny she was.'

'So she's thrown you over an' all.'

'She has, Fred. She cried, you know. It hurt her like hell but she threw me over. Where do you live?'

'Victoria Street.'

'Where's that?'

'Cressley Moor. You go out Bradford Road way.'

'I'll drop you off.'

'You're sure you're fit to drive?'

'Oh, yes. Have no fear. But I'll avoid the main roads, if you don't mind.'

'Drownin' your sorrows,' Fred said. 'It's no good, mate. You only feel twice as bad next day. I know. I've been doin' it on an' off for months. Fuckin' hell, but she's a bitch, is that Doris.' All animosity towards Frank seemed to have gone now that they were fellow victims.

'We were goin' to get wed, y'know, me an' Doris. Aye, we'd got that far. We'd've been grand an' comfortable an' all. I get good money in t'pit: twelve quid a week reg'lar, fifteen or sixteen if I strain me guts. That's more brass than her old feller ever saw at one time. A poor lot, Doris's family: ignorant sods. D'you ever meet any of 'em?'

'No, I never did.'

'No, she'd keep you well clear, I expect. You're not the sort they're used to at all. Not a bit. Make mincemeat of somebody like you. Shit you before breakfast. Have you got another job besides piano-playing?'

'I'm an accounts clerk.'

'No brass in that, is there?'

'Not much.'

'Can't you make a livin' from your playin'?'

'Doesn't seem like it.'

Frank was driving with great care, while trying not to

draw attention to himself by going too slow.

'What sort o' car's this?' Fred asked.

'MG. Bought it second-hand. Fourth-hand, actually.'

'Bonny. This Kane'll have a car, I expect?'

'Two. A midnight-blue Rolls Royce and a Triumph two-seater.'

'Fuck me. Loaded.'

'Loaded. A finger in every pie.'

'Includin' sweetie-pie,' Fred said, straight-faced. 'How many have you had tonight, mate?'

'Five pints, I think.'

'Five pints? I thought you were pissed.'

'I am pissed.'

'You can't be pissed on five pints. I've had twelve an' all I want to do is fart.'

'Don't fart in here, though, will you, Fred, there's a good lad. It's only a small car and I've a way to go when I've dropped you.'

'She's goin' up, is our Doris.' Fred said. 'Be singin' on t'wireless next, shouldn't wonder.'

'I wouldn't be surprised.'

'Be sleepin' out wi' them emperorsario fellers then, I reckon.' He nudged Frank. 'Was she good to you, mate?'

'Yes,' Frank said, 'she was good to me.'

'Aye, she was a warmhearted lass. Took cock like a real sweetheart.'

'And all in a good cause, of course,' Frank said. 'The advancement of Doris Preston.'

'Aye, she'll get on. Turn left here. I don't begrudge her, y'know. That's t'surprisin' thing about it. No, I call her. And you might. But I don't begrudge her. I couldn't have done all that for her. I'd only have held her back.'

'You're a very charitable man, Fred.'

'I enjoyed her while I had her, and now . . . well, I've got some good memories. Just here. Anywhere'll do. I live there.' Frank pulled in. 'I like you,' Fred said. 'I'm glad I saw you. I'd half a mind at one time to come round an' duff you up. If I'd come across you like tonight six months ago I'd more than likely have dropped you one on and started talking after. But you're a good lad, and we've both been done. Both of us . . .'

He rolled out and lifted himself off his hands and knees on the pavement.

'Careful if you're going up that entry, Fred.'

'Nay, lad, I've come up here more times bottled than sober.'

He lurched away into the darkness. The fart he'd been promising rang on the night air. There was no other sound for several seconds; then a loud metallic crash and a string of curses as Fred fell over a dustbin.

Frank waited until he heard a door shut behind the houses before driving away along the street. He was no longer sure where he was and would have to drive very carefully until he got his bearings.

Chapter Sixteen

He was smoking now, dropping his ash into a little coloured tin ashtray on the floor beside the bed. There was still no sign of Arny and he had heard no one go past to the top floor where Brenda slept. He got up and opened the window to empty the ashtray and let out the cigarette smoke. He switched off the light before getting back into bed and stretching himself on the strange mattress. As he fell asleep he was thinking of sunlight on the park lake and Rona in a summer frock.

Sunday

This young woman – a real doll, she is, a dish – this young woman is having her dinner in a café. The waiter brings her sweet course and she calls him back.

'Waiter,' she sez, 'this blancmange won't do.'

'Won't do, Madam?' sez the chap. 'Perhaps Madam would explain.' (A very high-class establishment, this. You can tell, can't you?) 'Perhaps Madam would explain.'

'It's not firm,' sez the dolly bird – and she was a dish, y'know, a real corker – 'It's not firm,' she sez. 'There are two things in life,' she sez, 'which I must have firm, and one of them is blancmange.'

Chapter Seventeen

Arny had one arm round Brenda's waist and she slumped against him as she shook with laughter. For a long time she had kept up her attitude of disdain, but several large gins and his persistent patter had gradually lowered her guard.

'I don't know where you get 'em all from. You could make a living on the pier.'

'And you could make a better one with that figure of yours than waiting-on in a boarding house.'

'How could I?'

'I know photographers in London who'd pay you good money just to stand still for them.'

'Pin-up stuff, you mean?'

'Pin-up stuff, modelling swimwear, lingerie – whatever they want you to do. You've got an asset there, girl, and you should be making the most of it.'

'How do you know so much? What do you do for a living?'

'I've got a partnership in a fruit-machine business. We hire 'em out to pubs and clubs, take a rent and a percentage of the takings.'

'You're living well on it,' she said sardonically.

'I didn't book this holiday,' Arny said. 'My cousin did. He doesn't think big like I do. But it's early days and I wasn't born with a silver spoon, so I won't make out I'm rolling in it. Not just yet. But in a couple of years we'll be coining it.'

'We shall have to pay a bob to get into the Metropole to see you then.'

'You exploit what you've got going for you and you'll have a suite at the Imperial.'

'I'm not doing so bad. I meet more people than I did in a mill in Oldham.'

'I've seen 'em,' Arny said. 'They're all on holiday from mills in Oldham, or shops in Leeds.'

'There's you.'

'There is, there is. And you want to take notice.'

He swung her gold-coloured dancing-shoes from the fingers of his free hand as they strolled up the quiet street of darkened houses. Only an occasional light shone on a ground floor.

'Christmas Day in the workhouse,' Arny said.

'You're in t'wrong quarter for night-clubs,' Brenda said.

'You've not always lived here, then?'

'Has anybody?'

'I don't know.'

'I came to help me Aunt Ginny. Her husband won a packet on the pools.'

'Did he now!'

'Aye. Of all the jammy devils. Allus wanted to live at the seaside, he said. But he didn't buy a bungalow where Ginny could sit back and put her feet up. Oh, no, he has to buy a boarding house and make her work even harder than she did before. Because he doesn't lift a finger himself. When he's not out supping he's on his back sleeping it off. Poor Ginny. She's slaved all her married life for that idle pig.'

'I get the impression you don't care for him.'

'I don't know how.'

'Why doesn't your auntie do a bunk?'

'In the first place, he holds the purse strings and in the second, I don't think in spite of it all she'd know what to do without him. Funny are folk, aren't they?'

'I have noticed.'

They came to the house and went up to the front door. As Brenda probed for the lock with her key, Arny took her arms and turned her round, pushing her gently but firmly into the corner of the porch.

'Don't be in such a hurry.'

He bent his head towards the pale shape of her face and kissed her, his arms sliding round her and drawing her to him. For a few moments she hung passively in his embrace; then as his desire charged her, her own arms came up round his neck and she strained herself to him along the length of her body, her lips parting under his to give him the thrust of her tongue. 'That's better,' he whispered, drawing back and letting her shoes fall as he ran his hands up from her waist and over her ribs, stopping just short of the blatant jut of her breasts.

'What a handy arrangement having our rooms so close. Did you put us in there on purpose?'

'What d'you mean?'

'Two young fellers. You might as well have 'em near, just in case.'

'Do you think I'm on the game up there, or what?' She put her hands on his chest and pushed him away. 'What makes you say a thing like that? I get on with me work and mind me own business.'

'You must have a chap, Brenda. A lass like you can't keep 'em *all* at arm's length.'

'I do, though. A damn' sight more than I encourage.'

'I'm privileged.'

'Not if you talk like that. Not if that's the kind of lass you think I am.' She tried to move past him. 'It's time I was going in. I can't lie in bed while somebody cooks my breakfast.'

'I've hurt your feelings,' Arny said, 'and that's the very last thing I wanted to do.'

'You shouldn't let your tongue run away with you.'

'I'm sorry, love. Will you give me another chance?'

'A chance to what? That's what I'd like to know.'

'Come with me for a swim tomorrow afternoon,' Arny said.

'You've had that. Sunday afternoon's when I catch up on all me little private chores.' She stood aside and let him in. 'You can find your way from here, can't you?'

'Where are you going?'

She pointed down the basement steps. 'Through the kitchen. I want to collect something.'

Arny kissed her again. She let him, but that was all.

'Till tomorrow night, then.'

'Who said owt about tomorrow night?'

'Think about where you'd like to go.'

She was a little taken aback when he went in and shut the door, leaving *her* standing there.

Chapter Eighteen

Truscott was dozing in an easy-chair in the dark kitchen. His wife had put out the light and left him there, hoping that he would not come to bed and disturb her as he snored and constantly shifted his bulk, and tried to fondle her in his dreams.

Brenda started as she switched on the light and saw him. She tried never to be alone with him and hoped now that she could get away before he woke.

The things she wanted were hanging on the bars of an airer up under the ceiling. She let it down on its rope as quietly as she could and removed a blouse and a petticoat and a couple of pairs of nylons, then fingered the other things there in search of something else.

'Been dancin', Brenda love?'

She started as Truscott spoke, and spun round. He lay in the chair in shirtsleeves, waistcoat open over his belly, and watched her with his small blue eyes. He saw the tremble of her breasts as she swung to face him and his throat thickened. She stood with her feet apart, a high colour in her face. He longed for her to walk the few steps to him and press his face against her breasts while she stroked his hair and murmured an invitation to her bed. 'Come with me. You shouldn't be sleeping down here. Come and cuddle up with me where it's cosy. It's time we got friendly, you and me. Time we had an arrangement. You'd like that, wouldn't you? I know from the way you look at me . . .' But all he could see as she faced him was a blaze of loathing. Why couldn't she be nice to him? It would make everything so easy.

She looked quickly again among the things on the airer, trying not to turn her back on him.

'Have you lost something, Brenda love?'

'It doesn't matter.' She hauled the airer back up and wound the rope round the wall cleat.

'Would it be these, by any chance?'

Truscott's hand was digging down into the chair, behind him. It came up holding a crumpled pair of her panties.

'What are you doing with them?' She watched as he pressed them against his face. 'You dirty bugger. Hand 'em over.' She started towards him but stopped again as he twisted in the chair then came to his feet. He held out his hand.

'I'll swap you for them you've got on.'

Brenda took quick stock of the situation. Any moment now he would think to get between her and the door to the stairs. And he could be upon her before she could re-open the street door, which was locked.

'Do you want to watch while I take 'em off?'

He stared at her. He could not believe it. She was actually lifting the hem of her skirt. Silken thighs appeared. The thought of what delight might come next, of all the delight that could be his if only she would be his pal, held him transfixed.

Then Brenda pounced, stabbing at him with a stiff-armed jab that threw him back against the chair and daring to grab his wrist and force her panties out of his fingers before fleeing for the stairs to the hall.

She slowed down as she climbed the three flights to her room. He would not follow her now, but she slid the bolt on the door before beginning to undress, scattering her clothes about the room.

She stood naked before the full-length glass in the wardrobe door. Fancying herself like this had become a habit and with Arny's praise fresh in her mind she was encouraged. Her brassiere had left red weals across her ribs. She needed a new one. Her breasts were bigger, but they still sagged hardly at all without support. She turned this way and that, admiring their thrust and the shallow dome of her belly and her rounded thighs. One day, she had always thought, her body would get her a man who would take her into a life of luxury and ease. Men needed one thing from a woman to make them happy. Or put it another way, they were ready to do almost anything to get it. Luckily she enjoyed giving it – to the right kind. Truscott made her flesh crawl, which she supposed was a pity because he was loaded. Arny, on the other hand, might not have much money now but she was sure he would in time. She didn't doubt that he was on his way: there was that something special about him that, now she remembered his hands on her and his confident smile, started the excitement moving in her stomach. She hoped as she settled into bed that he would not be long before he made his next move.

Chapter Nineteen

Arny sat up in bed with a grunt and massaged his scalp with his fingertips before reaching for cigarettes and lighter. The characteristic aroma of the first smoke of the day reached Frank who was standing, already partly dressed, at the window. A thin heat mist hung over the drab yards and pleasure stirred in him at the thought of seeing Rona again.

'Looks as if it could be warm today.'

'Hope so.'

'What time did you get in last night?'

'This morning. Getting on for one. You were well away.' Arny scratched reflectively at his scalp. 'Scurf,' he said. 'Can't get rid of it. I wash my hair regular and don't plaster it with goo, yet I get scurf.' He looked with distaste at his fingernails. 'You were working well last night, weren't you? I turn my back for ten minutes and you're fixed up with a bird.'

'Comes from Cressley, would you believe,' Frank said. 'Staying with an uncle and aunt in Marton.'

'Good-looker as well, if you like that kind.'

'Well, I do,' Frank said.

'Not too much all at once, though, eh?' Arny said.

'Just enough.'

'That's the ticket.'

Frank knew that he was being cautioned. He had been at the mercy of one girl only a little while ago. It was much too soon to let himself become dependent on another. All the same, he had no intention of trying to damp the glow of anticipation with which he had faced the day from the moment of waking up.

66

Chapter Twenty

Breakfast was a sprinkling of cornflakes in the bottom of a soup dish, followed by a strip of under-fried bacon, a fried egg and half a fried tomato.

'Morning, pet,' Arny said when Brenda came to serve them.

Her response was curt and impersonal.

'A night-bird, Brenda,' Arny said. 'Sings her sweetest after dark. Best stolen away from before dawn.'

'Did you make that much progress?'

'No. But enough.'

'I fixed up to see this girl again this afternoon,' Frank said. 'Is it going to leave you at a loose end?'

Arny shook his head. 'It fits in very nicely with what I had in mind.'

'Did you hear anything about a robbery in Cressley yesterday?' Frank asked him.

'Why? Something spectacular, was it?'

'No. Just that it happened at home. A cosh job. Pawnbroker's shop. Knocked the old chap out and cleaned out the till.'

'How come you know all about it?'

'Rona's uncle's a retired copper. He said it was in the evening paper.'

'Anybody "helping them with their enquiries"?'

'Not that he knew of.'

'There must be hundreds of cases where they get clean away with it. Tucked away in police files. Not a clue.'

'Didn't you run errands for a chap in Pym Street at one time, Arny?'

'Roundsley,' Arny said. 'Pawnbroker, jeweller. Why? Is that where—?'

'Pym Street,' Frank said.

'It must be him, then. But I thought there was nothing left of Pym Street.'

'So did I.'

They went out directly after breakfast, calling to buy Sunday papers before settling into the south-facing seat of a promenade shelter where they could enjoy the sun and still have a partial view of the beach and the sea.

'Here it is,' Frank said after a time. He shook out the folded the sheets of the newspaper. ' "Cressley, Yorks, Saturday. Police officers were still at the bedside late tonight of seventy-three-year-old Mr William Roundsley, who had not yet recovered consciousness after being beaten and robbed in his Pym Street pawnbroker's shop sometime around mid-day today. Mr Roundsley, who lives in premises at the rear of the shop, was found by a niece, Mrs G. Matthews, who had been helping him earlier in the morning and who returned to the shop at two p.m. It is not yet known exactly how much the unknown assailant got away with. Mrs Matthews, in an interview with our reporter, said she thought it would be a substantial sum and that she had often tried to impress upon her uncle the danger of keeping too much money in the shop. But, said Mrs Matthews, Mr Roundsley is a kindly man who looks upon all his customers as his friends, and he only laughed at her fears. The police have issued a request for all persons who were in the shop or its vicinity this morning to come forward as they may be able to help the investigation." '

' "A kindly man",' Arny said. 'He'd nip a currant in two. He kept a lot of money in the shop because he was lending it out at colossal rates of interest. And if you don't take your brass to the bank too often the tax man can only guess how much profit you're making.' He took the paper from Frank and skimmed the report in silence. 'I don't think they've a cat in hell's chance of finding who did it. He's probably sitting pretty miles away by now . . .'

'Perhaps reading about it in the papers,' Frank said. 'Wondering if he can have made a mistake somewhere after all; just one tiny slip that will lead them to him . . .'

Arny had turned a page and was looking at a picture of a film starlet more renowned for her mammary development than her ability to act.

'I like tits,' he said, 'but there's such a thing as moderation. Them must flop to her belly button when she takes the harness off.' He lowered the paper and gazed into the middle distance. 'Now you take Brenda . . .'

'I thought you'd staked a prior claim.'

'I have. You take hers. I'm ready to bet they hardly droop at all.'

'I never contradict a connoisseur.'

'No. And if everything goes like I'm hoping, I'll be able to tell you for sure by tea-time.'

Chapter Twenty-one

A clock ticked into the silence of the room. The little shabby man with the dewdrop under his nostrils listened to its beat and wondered if it had been thought out, something like the Chinese water torture. Almost as inexorable as the tick was the determination of the two men who faced him, watching him, waiting for him to speak. That the voice of the senior one, who had been doing the talking, was soft and insinuating did not comfort him. Whether they barked or pleaded, threatened or cajoled, their purpose was the same – to see him behind bars. At present he was still denying everything and would go on doing so until he saw an advantage in owning up. What he could not understand, what his mind would not grasp, was why on this occasion they were being quite so determined, quite so relentless in their desire to make him come clean. It was as though they were playing the game to new rules, and he didn't yet know what they were.

Again the first one spoke, breaking the silence, covering the tick of that damned clock.

'Now you can't deny that we nabbed you fair and square last night, can you, old man?'

'I'm sayin' nothin' without legal advice.'

The first time the little man had said this it had brought a flicker of humour into the grey eyes watching his face. Now it produced a marked glint of impatience.

'You'll get all the legal advice you need when the time comes. But before that we want you to tell us exactly where you got this wallet.' He pointed to the notecase lying on the table between them. 'That's all we want to know, but it'll go easier with you if you stop arsing about and tell us now, not a week next Thursday. Now.'

The little man's eyes watered profusely but his mouth was set in a thin obstinate line. The senior man sighed and glanced at his colleague. He nodded and strolled into a corner behind the little man. The detective-sergeant fixed the man with a hard unblinking stare.

'Look at me, Fleetwood, you mangy little cunt.'

'There's no need for that, Mr Ransome.'

'But there is, you snot-gobbling little shit-bag. And I'm telling you here and now that if you don't level with us you're going away for ten years.'

'What you tryin' to give me? They don't hand out tenners for dipping.'

'They do for robbery with violence, you bone-brained little twat. And that's what the owner of this wallet's got coming to him. Why do you keep insisting that it's your property? Are you too fucking dumb to come in out of the rain?'

'I ain't done no robbery with. What're you trying to do to me?'

The other man came back round the table and motioned his colleague aside. Ransome, whose face was now the colour of violence, looked disappointed.

'Now listen. Open that stupid and devious little mind of yours and listen to what I say, because my patience is at an end. Listen and look. Among the banknotes in this wallet – which you keep on saying is yours – are four brand new one-pounders. Right? The numbers run consecutively. See? What do you notice about them? Don't strain yourself, I'll tell you. There's a gap in the row – one number missing. See? Now, we know where that other note, the one with the missing number, is. The West Riding CID have it over in Wakefield. And do you know where they found it? They found it by the unconscious body of a shopkeeper who had been coshed and robbed in his premises in Cressley by a person or persons unknown on Saturday morning. And they have a witness who says that these notes were in the till with the other one.'

The little man's truculence was evaporating fast.

'I've never been to any place called Cressley.'

'You can thank your lucky stars we believe that,' the CID man said grimly. 'Now we've larked about long enough. Come clean and tell us all you know about the wallet and who you lifted it from.'

Fleetwood 'came clean'.

Chapter Twenty-two

'You're an only child, then?'

'Yes.'

'Both you and Arny?'

'Huh huh.'

'Who was related?'

'Our fathers were brothers.'

She relaxed on her elbow beside him. He was very, very conscious of the scent of her as she moved. Just down the slope was the lake. There were a number of rowing-boats out. In the bandstand by the landing-stage a military band in uniforms with glinting chainmail at the shoulders were tuning their instruments.

'I've got two brothers and a sister,' Rona said.

'Have you really?' Frank said. 'I'd assumed you were an only one as well.'

'Why? Have you got some way of spotting them?'

'Well, it's obviously not to be relied on, whatever it is; but I'd got you down as the single treasured issue of some gentle and perfect union.'

'Crikey!'

'Late issue, of ageing parents.'

'You're not far off there, because I'm the youngest and the last.'

'That might explain it.'

'Any minute now you're going to say I've obviously been spoilt—'

'I'm not going to say any such thing. It was more of a compliment than that.'

'Well, I don't think you're a tinsel-tongued

skirtchaser, so you must be an old-fashioned romantic.'

'I can't deny it.'

'But I ought to warn you: don't start building a pedestal for me. I get dizzy.'

'I beg your pardon.'

'I'm very flattered all the same, so don't go to the other extreme and start dragging me about by the hair, so to speak.'

'Just strike the happy medium, is that it?'

'Something like that.' She pulled at the short grass, 'I mean, I am getting the correct drift of all this, I hope. We have suddenly come quite a long way in quite a short time . . .?'

'We have. We have indeed.'

'Because if I've got it wrong I'll have no option but to leave you and find a corner to blush in.'

'Why don't we reassure each other?' Frank said.

'I'm all for that.'

Frank went down on his own elbow, turning to face her. She was looking at his mouth, her eyes hooded. He moved his head in and touched with the lightest of contact. She brought her free hand up behind his head before shifting her supporting arm and taking him down with her.

'This isn't really my style,' she said, 'necking on the grass in a public place; but sometimes you have to make an exception.'

74

Chapter Twenty-three

Arny returned from the corner shop where he had gone
to buy the rest of the Sunday papers. No one saw him as
he went up the stairs to the room. He took off his jacket
and draped it carefully on a hanger. He loosened his tie
and opened the papers on the bed. He scanned them one
after the other without finding what he was looking for,
then folded them again, neatly. He lit a cigarette and
stood at the open window. The air was still and warm.
He hoped that he was not wasting this afternoon of glori-
ous weather by hanging about inside for nothing.
Brenda came out of a door below and carried a card-
board packing-case across to one of the outhouses. He
shifted his position and craned his neck to watch her,
wondering whether he should call down and let her
know he was there. Waiting.

He moved from the window and pulled his case from
under the bed. He lifted it on to the bed, unlocked it and
opened the lid. He had left a few clothes in there and
from under them he took out a thick roll of banknotes. He
glanced at the door and went and slipped the catch
before setting out the notes in little heaps of ten on the
counterpane. His mouth moved in the faintest sketch of a
smile as he scraped them together again and replaced
the rubber band. From under the clothes in the case now
his hand emerged holding a revolver with a stubby barrel. His face became thoughtful as he stood up and
weighed the weapon in his palm. He held the gun, working his palm on the butt, feeling the satisfaction of it in
his hand.

Suddenly throwing off his mood, he swung the gun up to point at the door and went into a gunfighter's crouch. 'Bang! Bang!' With a grin he returned both money and gun to the case. He put the newspapers in, too, before locking it again and pushing it back under the bed.

He went silently out on to the landing and looked down between the banisters to the ground floor. The only sound now was the faint chink of crockery as someone set the tables in the dining-room for the next meal. Presently, the front door opened and closed with a crash and a heavy person with creaking shoes passed along the hall. Arny heard Mrs Truscott's voice, sharp and peevish, unguarded in the assumption that all her boarders were out of doors: 'How many times have I told you not to come through the front door in that condition?' A man's voice, slurred and indistinct, said something in return. 'Do you think *I* care if you break your neck down the steps?' Mrs Truscott shrilled at him. 'Good riddance, I'd say.' Truscott was home from his lunchtime session at the boozer.

Chapter Twenty-four

'Do you know Radley Street?'

'No.'

'You'd know Monkwood Pit, though?'

'Isn't that closed down now?'

'Yes. And old Radley Street itself is gone too. It was a couple of parallel rows of terrace houses, two up, two down, running up to a fence of railway sleepers with the pit on the other side. It had a particularly foul slagheap; or it had when I was a child and it was still burning. In wet weather it stank awful. I was born with that stink in my nostrils.'

The women of the neighbourhood had been more bothered by the everlasting grit and coal dust that blew off the stack in an invisible cloud, robbing lace curtains of their freshness in no time and settling back in a duster's flick on to newly polished surfaces.

The family group had been small: just his father and mother, Uncle Vernon, Aunt Carrie, Arny. His mother was not a local girl: his father had brought her back with him from a spell in the Derbyshire coalfield.

'My father never worked at Monkwood. My mother used to rib him about it. "A pit on the doorstep," she'd say, "and you travel a thre'penny bus-ride!"'

His father and mother . . . He had never really understood how it was with them. More often than not he would hear them before he opened the door. Having another row. Then if he was alone, and there was no neightbour to see him hover on the step and turn away, and if it was not pouring with rain, he would sometimes pass another five or six minutes in a circuit of the nearby streets, hoping to give them time to calm down. But often he could not avoid breaking in on them, when his mother was helpless in a frenzied eruption of rage, her eyes flashing green fire at his father, sitting at the table, sullen and silent until his more slowly kindled temper gave him voice also. There might have been, he had thought much later, some vast incurable grievance behind it all, but the thing he had never understood at the time was how such monumental rows could appear to be about things so unimportant. It seemed that for them rowing was one half of life. They were incapable of living in quiet harmony. When they were not loving each other to the exclusion of all else they had to quarrel. Sometimes then his father would turn to him and they would go off together, to the pictures, to a football match, or just for a walk over the fields. And these were bitter-sweet times for Frank, because when the quarrel died, as it always did, his father and mother would draw together ever closer, a pair, man and woman, whole and complete, with no one else in the world but the two of them.

'Was she pretty?' Rona asked.

'I thought so later, in a thin, fine-drawn way. All skin and bone and nerve-endings. I think I might have a photograph.' He took out his wallet. 'Yes. They don't always put over the real person, unfortunately. This was taken on his embarkation leave.'

'Was he called up? Weren't coal miners exempt?'

'He volunteered. For some reason, he chose to go. My mother screamed at him. Her rage that day was truly awesome. She thought he'd rejected her. It was the only way she could see it: that he wanted to get away from her. Perhaps there was some truth in it. He'd been given the opportunity of a breather, a fresh perspective. She never really forgave him.'

'Funny,' Rona said, holding the photograph. 'Funny to think they were not all that much older than we are now.'

'No, that's right.'

'Which of them do you take after?'

'Haven't you seen enough to know?'

'It's all your father so far. I'd be sorry to think your mother hadn't left her mark somewhere.'

Ah, but did she guess what kind of waywardness had come with the fire?

'Perhaps it comes out in the music,' Rona said.

'Perhaps so.'

'Not the most likely of backgrounds to throw up a talented musician.'

'No.'

'Was there a piano in the house?'

'Oh, no; the piano was Aunt Carrie's. She played a bit, mostly for chapel functions. She'd have liked Arny to take it up, but he had no interest. When she saw I was drawn to it she encouraged me and gave me my first lessons.'

It had been the period of greatest harmony between Frank and his aunt, when she satisfied some need in herself by trying to show that she could provide a better home for him than the one he came from. His mother was on war-work and shifts. When she worked nights he slept at Arny's. That was how he came into the house that day, quietly as always so as not to disturb her morning sleep, and, as he crept upstairs, heard sounds that drew him to the partly open door of her room.

The sounds were his mother's gasps and little cries above the rhythmic creak of the bed on which, upright and naked, her back arched, she straddled and rode the supine body of a man who Frank could only think for a heart-stopping moment must be his father, come home without warning. Until his furtive return down the stairs brought him to the overcoat hanging behind the door: a coat of grey herringbone tweed with patch pockets; a coat Frank had admired when he had seen it on a man waiting at the end of the street at dusk.

Chapter Twenty-five

Arny was lying on his bed blowing smoke rings at the cracked plaster of the ceiling when the creak of a stair brought him to his feet. The door stood an inch ajar and looking out he saw Brenda turn the corner and go on up to her room. He waited and watched. In a few minutes she returned, wearing a pale-blue belted wrap and carrying a towel and what looked like a bundle of stockings and smalls. The sound of the bolt on the bathroom door carried plainly to him as, leaving the door ajar, he lay down again and flipped with only a part of his attention through the pages of a *Melody Maker* which Frank had brought with him.

In half an hour Brenda came back. As soon as he had seen her pass Arny slipped out of his shirt and got a clean one from the drawer. With his pocket knife he loosened the thread holding a button and pulled the button off. He put the shirt on and went out and up the short flight of stairs to Brenda's door where he knocked softly. There was a short delay before she opened the door a crack and peered out.

'Oh, it's you.'

'Were you expecting somebody else?'

She opened the door a little wider but still kept one shoulder behind it. 'I thought everybody had gone out.'

'I think they all have, except me. I, er, need a woman's help.'

'For what?'

He showed her the pearl button in the palm of his hand. 'If you've got a needle and thread we're in business.'

For a few seconds she looked him over. He returned the look, his eyes bland and free of guile. Then she turned away.

'All right. Come in.'

He followed her into the room and sat down on the rigid edge of her narrow bed.

'Make yourself at home,' she said, glancing over her shoulder.

'Just testing.' He grinned broadly as she turned her head again.

The room had a sloping ceiling and the dormer window was set so high that Arny could see only sky through it. It was a bigger room than the one he and Frank were occupying but it had the same cheap furniture and the same impersonal austerity. She looked to have done little to make it her own.

'Come to the light.'

She turned with needle and thread and he walked round the foot of the bed and stood before her under the high window. There was not a wisp of cloud to be seen in the blue spread of sky.

He looked at Brenda's bowed head. Her hair was darker in the roots and ready for another treatment of whatever she used to blonde it. He began to think about the colour of the hair at her crotch and felt himself begin to stiffen.

'Where's your friend this afternoon?'

'Run out on me. Found himself a girl.'

'Quick worker.'

'Not as quick as me.'

'I'll bet there's not many are.'

With a few cross-strokes she finished fastening the button and snapped off the thread.

'There you are. You can go now before you get me talked about.'

'You'd never forgive me if I did.' He looked at her as she frowned. 'Went,' he said.

'God, you're sure of yourself, aren't you?'

She put the needle and thread aside and used both

hands to draw her wrap closer. Her action tautened the rayon over the high points of her breasts. Arny stretched out his arm and drew his forefinger lightly over one already hardening nipple and watched Brenda's face as her eyes closed in something longer than a blink.

'What d'you think you're doing?'

'Trying to find out what pleases.'

He put out his other hand. Both forefingers traced circles round the stiffened tips of her breasts. Still he kept his arms' length, willing her to come to him. Only when, her eyes closed now, she swayed on her feet did he step forward and slide his arm round her and draw her in, his other hand finding cold skin inside her wrap. She shuddered.

'How long have we got?' he asked.

'Long enough for all you're getting.'

'What do you mean?'

'If you think I'm going to risk you putting me in the club, and you away to London . . .'

'There's no need for all that.'

'I think there is.'

'Look.' He showed her the condom in his hand.

'You cheeky sod.'

'Aren't you glad, though?'

'You're still not there, so don't get clever about it.'

'Let me look at you,' Arny said. He parted her wrap and put both hands on the moulded hardness of her breasts. 'I knew they were wonderful,' he said. She was trembling without restraint now. 'Come on,' he said. 'Come and lie down and let me persuade you.'

He was quite a while before he eased himself over her and made an entry. By that time she could hardly breathe with the waiting and her nails bit deep into his back.

Chapter Twenty-six

'Why don't you stay and have your tea with us?' Rona's aunt asked Frank. 'You're very welcome.'

'Yes, do, Frank,' Rona said. 'Could you?'

'Well, thanks. I'd love to and I'm sure I'm not missing out on anything splendid at the digs—'

'I'm certain you're not,' Mrs Rogers said. 'Standards must have gone up while I wasn't looking if they can match my table.'

'Well, they haven't at Mrs Truscott's anyway,' Frank said. 'But it's my cousin I'm thinking about. I ought to check up on him at least and let him know what I'm doing.'

'If you're going to a concert at Southport you'll barely have time as it is,' Rona's uncle said. He had just got up from his Sunday afternoon nap and lounged in self-indulgent ease in a fireside chair. 'Hop over the estuary and you'd be there in quicksticks, but you've got to go inland and come back out again.'

'Perhaps we'd better forget it,' Frank said. 'It looked so tempting from the poster, but if we were late or couldn't get in when we got there . . .'

'Playing something interesting, are they?'

'Some Brahms, some Richard Strauss.'

'Strauss, eh?'

'Richard, Uncle Len, not Johann,' Rona told him.

'Rona says you play yourself,' Rogers said.

'Mostly jazz, though.'

'I used to do a bit with the amateur operatics when I was younger.'

'Oh, yes. Baritone, were you?'

'Ah, you're being misled by my size. No, I sang tenor. I never did a lot of big parts but I didn't have a bad voice, if I do say so myself.'

'Now, Len,' his wife said.

'Come on, Olive, you know I had a good voice.'

'You had. But you shouldn't blow your own trumpet in front of a visitor.'

'If you've summat to blow your trumpet about, then get to know when to blow it,' Rogers said. 'That's what I always say. Take this young chap here – our Rona says he's a first-rate pianist – marvellous was the word she used – but you wouldn't know it from the way he sits there and says nothing.'

'Why should he walk about braggin'?' Rona's aunt said. 'If he can play the piano, them that need to know will know. Why should he go about braggin' about it?'

'You don't understand my meaning, Olive,' Rogers said, 'so let's change the subject. I've just remembered I've something to tell you.'

'What about, as if I can't guess?'

'About this pawnshop robbery in Cressley we were talking about last night.'

'Have they caught somebody for it?'

'Not yet. But they've got a lead on it right here in Blackpool.'

'Here?' Rona said. 'What kind of a lead?'

'I had a lunchtime pint with Derek Ransome. Detective-Sergeant Ransome, CID, an old colleague of mine.'

'Do you ever drink with anybody else but old colleagues?' Rona's aunt asked.

'Listen, Olive, this is interesting. It seems they picked a chap up last night. Not for the first time. Regular small-time thief, works the promenade at rush times, picking pockets. I know him meself. Anyway, he had a wallet on him when they brought him in. Hadn't had time to drop it, I suppose. It had some new one-pound notes in it. It seems them notes tally with one found on the floor of the shop in Cressley after the robbery. The old man had a niece in helping that morning and she remembers taking the note with four others, all in sequence. They sent out word to watch for those notes. A bit of a long shot them all turning up together like that, eh?'

'I haven't quite got this,' Frank said. 'There must be other notes in the same sequence. Banks quite often issue large amounts in new notes like that. For a firm's wages, for instance.'

'Agreed,' Rogers said, 'and these notes very likely did come straight out of somebody's wage packet.'

'But look,' Frank said, 'Cressley's on holiday this week. There could be any number of people from that same factory or mill walking about Blackpool with notes bearing the same sequence of numbers.'

'But don't you see,' Rogers said, edging his bulk forward on to the edge of his seat and leaning towards Frank, 'we're talking about four notes in a seqence of five, that's all. The missing one isn't from either end. If it was it could be the beginning of a new sequence or the end of the sequence before. No, this single note comes from the middle of the four. Which means there's no doubt at all that the notes in this wallet were in the shop yesterday morning.'

'But the man they arrested isn't the man they want, is he?' Rona asked.

'Oh, no. No, robbery with violence isn't his style, thief though he is. No, the man they want is the one he took the wallet from between seven and eight last night.'

'Oh, my goodness,' Rona said, 'isn't that suddenly exciting?'

'But that's funny—' Frank began, then stopped.

'What's funny?' Rona asked.

'Oh, nothing . . . He got to Blackpool rather quickly, didn't he?'

'Hundreds of others did it. You did it yourself. He could have travelled on the same train as you, for all you know.'

'So they know the man they want was in Blackpool last evening, but nothing more?' Rona said.

'That's about the size of it. He was a young chap,' Fleetwood said, smartly set up. Blackpool's full of 'em.'

Frank's heart seemed to contract in a spasm that almost stopped his breath. The room had become oppressively warm. That fire . . . Why must they have a fire after such a day?

From somewhere outside the haze he heard Rogers say, 'You don't look so cracky, young feller. Been over-doing the sun a bit today?'

Frank put his hand to his forehead, partly to hide his face, which he was sure Rogers would be able to read. 'I think perhaps I have. And smoking too many cigarettes.'

'For heaven's sake,' Rona's aunt said, 'let me give you a cup of tea. Why don't you telephone your lodgings and ask them to give your cousin a message?'

'Yes,' Frank said. 'Yes, I think I will. Thanks.'

Chapter Twenty-seven

He knew that she was aware of the change in him, and troubled by it. He felt tainted by his suspicion, a different person, no longer entitled to the growing joy in her company, and he could not find words to reassure her. So what could she do but blame some shortcoming in herself?

They had given up the concert and settled for a film in town. Frank walked her home once again and was driven deeper into silence the more he searched for saving small-talk.

'Aren't you feeling so good?' Rona asked.

'I've got a headache,' he lied.

He should have made excuses at tea-time, he thought; pleaded fairness to Arny. He realised now that he could have gone off on his own, whereas at the time the only alternative to staying with Rona had seemed to lie in facing Arny before he had thought it all out.

She let go of his arm to walk round some people and did not take it again.

'Frank . . .'

'Hmmm?'

'We don't *have* to travel as fast as we seemed to be doing.'

'What d'you mean?'

'I mean we can slow down, mark time, let everything catch up with us.' She added in a moment when he did not respond, 'Even second thoughts.'

'Do you always read something . . . ominous into a quiet mood?'

'I won't if you tell me not to. But you will have to tell me, because I'm not as sure of myself as you might think I am.'

He took her hand and squeezed it, drawing her arm through his.

'Are you telling me now?'

'Yes.'

'I won't ask you any more, then. Except . . .'

'What?'

'If you've got something on your mind and there's any way I can help, I wish you'd let me know.'

'All right.'

'You will remember, won't you?'

'Yes.'

'And if you want to get some air, have a breather, so to speak, there's plenty of time. I don't go home for another ten days.'

'Can I phone you tomorrow?'

'Of course you can.'

It would be all right. Once he saw Arny he would know it. One look at Arny's face was all he needed.

Chapter Twenty-eight

But Arny did not come in that night.

Monday

There was this honeymoon couple on their wedding night at Blackpool. He's in bed – waiting – and she's at the window, looking out.

'What do you find so fascinating out there, Mavis, love?' the bridegroom asks her.

'It's the Tower,' she sez.

'What about the Tower?' her husband asks.

'I'm just admiring how big and straight it stands.'

'Well you just come to bed now, love,' he sez. 'That'll still be standing in the morning.'

Chapter Twenty-nine

The telegram had arrived in the evening while Frank was in. His mother was working dayshift now and the boy had had to come back. They had never had a telegram that Frank could remember and he thought his mother must have known what it was as soon as she saw the lad on the step. She didn't open it at once, but turned it over and over in her hands and looked at it. When at last she had read it she crumpled it and let it fall before opening the door to the stairs and running up without a word. Frank picked up the paper, and smoothed it out on the table top under the window. For a moment his heart seemed to stop beating altogether. Mrs Denshaw from the house opposite was standing on her step as she did on fine evenings. She would have seen the boy and soon the news would be all through the surrounding streets. Frank sat down and put his head in his hands, moaning a little before he let sobs come, racking him at first, then quietening into a steady desperate weeping.

That night he went into his mother's room when he heard her crying. He turned back the clothes and slipped in beside her, into his father's half of the double bed, and as she felt him there she turned over and drew him fiercely to her. 'Oh, Frank. Whatever shall we do without him?'

For a while after that it was as if she could not bear to let him out of her sight. Then one evening he found the house empty. His mother did not come in till after midnight and from then on it was as it had always been since his father went away.

Four months after the telegram came his mother and a man were pulled out of the wreckage of a motor car on the Leeds–York road. The man lived another twelve hours but Frank's mother was dead when they got her to hospital. Afterwards Frank wondered if it had been the man in the grey tweed overcoat with the patch pockets. He never saw him again, anyway.

He went to live with Uncle Vernon, Aunt Carrie – and Arny.

Chapter Thirty

He woke at six-thirty and looked across at Arny's undisturbed bed. There was no escape now: sleep had assembled the evidence into an irrefutable pattern of guilt.

The robbery had taken place just before the lunch-hour – say twelve-thirty. Seven or eight minutes' brisk walk from Pym Street to the railway station. They had caught the twelve-forty-two and Arny had only just made it. Arny had lost his wallet around seven-thirty in the evening. He had not wanted to report it to the police. He had said they would not be able to do much; but it was unlike him not to want to try to make somebody pay. His attitude on Sunday morning, when they discussed the robbery, had been almost too casual, especially as he had once known the shopkeeper. A thief with local knowledge . . .

He tried for a moment to clutch at the thought that more than one person from Cressley could have had his wallet stolen around the same time, and then asked himself how far he could expect coincidence to stretch.

Where would the money be if Arny had done it? Where else but in his suitcase?

Look in the suitcase and prove yourself wrong, he told himself. Look in the case and you'll know for the rest of your life that you thought Arny capable of it.

'He is,' something said in his mind.

'No.'

'Yes.'

In an abrupt movement Frank threw back the

bedclothes and swung his feet to the floor. He crouched and pulled the case from under Arny's bed. It was locked. He got his keys and tried that belonging to his own case, easing it in and out a hair's breadth at a time until it engaged and turned. He lifted the lid and saw the newspapers. He took them out and moved aside the clothes left in the case. He found the roll of notes at once and tried telling himself that it was a reserve, left there for safety. Except that it was far too much for a week's holiday. He looked at the roll, trying to estimate the amount there, and his other hand, still probing, felt the shape of the revolver.

He lifted it clear of the case and sat back on his bed, the roll of notes in one hand, the gun in the other. He shut his eyes and heard himself repeating in frantic horror, 'Oh, God, oh God! Oh Christ! Oh, my God!'

When Arny spoke to him from the doorway, startling him, all the feeling in Frank seemed to channel into fury.

'Find anything interesting?'

'You fool. You bloody stupid fool.' Frank held out his hands as though offering the money and the gun to Arny. 'You must have been raving mad, Arny. You must have been out of your mind.'

'Cool it,' Arny said. He pushed the door to with his stockinged foot. He was carrying his shoes and his jacket. He dropped them on the bed, took the money and the weapon from Frank, returned them to the case, locked the case and slid it back under the bed.

'Wasn't it locked?'

Frank shrugged and indicated his own keys on the bed beside him.

'What made you go into it?' Frank made no reply. 'You found what you were looking for, didn't you? You knew something, didn't you?' He sat down on the other bed and took hold of Frank's wrists. 'What put you on to me, Frank?'

'The police picked up the bloke that swiped your wallet. It seems there were some new banknotes in it and they tallied with one found in the shop.'

'How do you know all this?'

'Rona's uncle. He got it from a friend on the force.'

Arny's grip tightened. 'You didn't say anything about me, did you?'

'No. Something made me clam up straight away.'

'You must have mentioned it already to the girl. In idle conversation.'

'No, for some reason it never came up.'

'You must have found plenty to talk about,' Arny said abstractedly. 'So they're no wiser?' he said in a minute.

'No. I find it hard to take in myself.' He felt stupid with knowledge. 'For God's sake, Arny, *why did you do it?*'

'Because I needed the money,' Arny said with mild, off-hand impatience. 'Why else?' He smacked his clenched right fist into his other palm. 'Christ, what luck, though! How much have they on me? Think hard, Frank. How much do they know?'

'All they really know is that you – the man they want – was in Blackpool on Saturday night.'

'That's right,' Arny said. 'How can they know anything else? They can't trace the wallet to me. It was an old one' – he smiled – 'I lost my good one in London ten days ago. Isn't that rich? – and there was nothing in this one except the dough. I don't know if they can take fingerprints off leather but it doesn't matter because they haven't got mine. No. They wouldn't even know this much if that stupid twat hadn't put his fingers in my pocket.'

'You should all wear a badge or a special tie,' Frank said, 'then you'd know one another.'

'Now just a minute, mate!' Arny's temper flashed only to subside at once as he glanced slyly at Frank, sitting hunched on the edge of his bed. 'All right, all right. No need to fly off the handle. You had me worried for a minute or two, that's all.'

'I'd worry,' Frank burst out. 'What about the old man you slugged? I wonder if he's worrying.'

'For fuck's sake,' Arny said, 'keep your voice down. Do you want the whole house to hear? Look, Frank, I'd no intention of hitting him, but he was running. Another few seconds and he'd have been out the back yelling blue murder. I thought I'd just tapped him.'

'But why did you have to do the job in the first place? I thought we'd both grown out of that lightfingered phase.'

'I've told you – I needed the money. You've heard me mention a guy called Norrie. I do a bit with him on the fruit-machines. I got the figures wrong one time and ended up owing him. He's been putting the bite on.'

'You mean you tried fiddling him and got your fingers burned. So to square that you've moved on to robbery with violence. Where's it going to end, Arny? Can't you see you're just getting in deeper and deeper?'

'Pay Norrie off and I'm in the clear. He sees that I don't stick fast and he'll know he can rely on me.'

'Give yourself up, Arny. They'll be lenient with you. It's your first offence.'

'What the hell are you talking about? This isn't nicking sweets from the corner shop. They'll put me away.'

'Give yourself up before they get you.' In his present state of mind Frank had an almost total belief in the efficiency of the police.

'How can they get me? It's pure chance that's got them so far.'

Frank got up and began abstractedly to collect his clothes. Then he turned on Arny.

'Look, don't you feel sorry for what you've done? I mean haven't you any conscience about it?'

'What's conscience, Frank? Something that tells you you'll be found out? Well I won't be found out. I didn't mean to hit the old man, but now it's done and giving myself up won't help anybody.'

'It would help you to start afresh.'

'Where have you got all this high-minded shit from, Frank? Is it something you've picked up lately? Do you really expect me to walk out of here and tell them I did it?'

'I don't know what I expect. I just know that I'm sick and scared.'

'What have you got to be scared about?'

'I'm scared for you.'

'You don't have to be. Just keep your mouth shut and there's nothing to be scared about.'

'In the meantime I'll try to get used to having a cosh-boy in the family.'

Arny flushed. 'Watch your mouth, Frank.'

Chapter Thirty-one

Brenda was in the basement kitchen. Following Arny downstairs, she had been drawn to his door by the sound of voices and a sudden irresistible curiosity to know if he was telling his cousin what they had been doing together. She had realised then that the two men were quarrelling. Brenda had keen ears and what had reached them while she stood on the landing was enough to touch a chord of memory. Now, after a search through the crumpled pages of the Sunday papers, she had found what she was looking for: a report of a robbery which had caught her eye only because the incident had taken place in the town Arny had come from.

As she remembered the night and added what she knew of Arny now her stomach churned with excitement. 'You've got a body to drive a man mad,' he had said as she lay under his gaze. She could have said the same of him some time later when she was almost weeping on the precipice of climax.

Who better to take her out of her aunt's boarding house and into a new and exciting life? He had guts; he had brains. He wouldn't stand still.

Less than a week left. Was it long enough for her to clinch it; to make him see that he couldn't do without what she had to offer?

She was still standing under the window with the sheet of newspaper in her hand when her aunt came in.

'I wish I'd time to read the paper in a morning. Haven't you even got the kettle on? I can't start the day till I've had my first cup of tea. And what are you shivering for? It's not cold, is it? You're not starting a cold, are you?'

Chapter Thirty-two

He could forget it for seconds at a time, in the act of cutting through a sausage, the need to blow his nose, the sound of a man's phlegmy morning cough from another table. These were the harmless, the normal things of normal yesterday. When your world disintegrated surely these things were shattered too? But no; a man coughed in the morning, noses needed to be blown, people ate – even Arny who, at this moment, was indistinguishable from these dull, normal, honest people around him, his hands, like theirs, moving over a plate, holding a knife and fork, with nothing at all about them to show that they had known the feel of a gun aimed in a blow at an old man's unguarded head.

Where was it that he had not seen it? Had the child's mischief, in which he himself had often participated, been in Arny's case the seeding of adult viciousness? Tell me, Arny, he thought. Tell me why. Not that you needed the money, that somebody was pressing you. Tell me really why, how.

But he didn't speak. Neither had uttered a word to the other since entering the room. Only when they got up together as usual and Frank made at once for the front door did Arny half-turn from the foot of the stairs and restrain him with a curt query:

'Going out?'

Their glances met, and, strangely, it was Frank's which faltered first.

'I thought I'd go for a walk.'

'By yourself?' Arny came to his side. 'Don't go and do anything silly, will you?'

Frank stepped away from him, still avoiding his eyes, and went out into the bright morning, down past houses just beginning to disgorge their patrons into another day of pleasure and out of the street by the corner shop where the leaves of newspapers stirred and lifted in the light breeze and the colours of the picture postcards were gaudy in the sun. He bought a paper and looked all through before he found a small paragraph on the front page. It said the police had reason to believe that a man they wished to question had been in Blackpool on Saturday night. The old man had still not recovered enough to make a statement.

He crossed the road and walked until he came out on to the Promenade and felt the breeze from the sea flap his trouser-legs and blow fresh and clean on his face. He made for Central Pier and, paying his toll, went through the turnstile and walked along the boards. It was early and there were plenty of seats and chairs to choose from. He walked well out towards the end of the pier and settled down in a corner of a shelter, looking across the low-tide sweep of sand to the white superstructure and latticed steelwork of the North Pier. He lit a cigarette and allowed his mind to wander.

He was not alone there. People began to stroll by: elderly couples coming to settle down for the morning; young men in small, high-spirited groups; girls arm-in-arm in pairs, wearing flowered dresses and white shoes, white handbags hanging from their wrists. Some were pretty and arrogant, others pathetic in the way they had dressed themselves like sacrificial offerings, waiting for some young chap to take the bait. But it was life: normal life. Sometimes there would be a young couple, also arm-in-arm, sometimes with their arms thrown round each other, safe from hometown killjoys. And children scampered by, small feet stamping the boards, their laughter and excited shrieks hanging on the sunny morning. Gradually the seats round Frank filled up. Some of the people settled down in silence; some greeted unexpected acquaintances who in this chance meeting seemed more like friends. Some wrote snappy sentences on the backs of postcards and licked stamps with which to despatch them.

Frank sat there and watched, only half-seeing most of the time, and only confusedly thinking as images and impressions and half-forgotten memories moved through his mind. But always at the centre of them, immovable, inescapable, was the rock-hard core of his present knowledge and always, as his mind wandered, it was there waiting, each time returning sharper, clearer, more terrible than before.

The sky to the south began to darken as the morning wore on and after a couple of hours Frank got up, leaving a litter of cigarette ends, and walked back to the Promenade as the rain clouds gathered and the breeze stiffened.

He remembered how, when he was small, he had accidentally broken a large looking-glass while alone in the house. The sudden awful prospect of seven years of bad luck had brought him to tears. He remembered how he had waited on his own for a long time, afraid to stir out of the house, forgetting for seconds at a time, only to face again and again those fragments of glass and their terrible portent for the future. And he remembered how sweet was his parents' homecoming with their boozily tolerant forgiveness for the glass itself and their laughing dismissal of his fears. He had felt like someone reprieved. But there would be no reprieve this time, no laughing Arny, the Arny of old, to greet him on his return to the house with the assurance that the gun and the money had never existed, that he had been living in a waking nightmare and the robbery was, like all the others, no more to them than a square of type on the page of a newspaper, a paragraph in someone else's life.

No. It was done. There was nothing more certain in the world.

Something made him glance back. He thought for a moment he saw Arny behind him. Imagination. He wandered aimlessly along the Promenade. There was nowhere to go, nothing to do. He could not return to the house before lunchtime, and he did not want to go back then. A blast of music drew him to the door of an amusement arcade. He went in and got change for half a crown from the jingling palm of a key-festooned attendant. For the next hour he clattered ball-bearings into holes behind the glass fronts of wall machines, shot metal cats off painted walls with ball-bearing bullets, heard the sniggers of the lads bent over their penny peep at 'My Lady's Toilet' and felt the amplified roar of the jukebox beat against his ear-drums. And in the middle of it all he was alone in the desert of his knowledge.

Chapter Thirty-three

The weather broke towards lunchtime. Day-trippers had packed into the town during the morning. As Frank walked back to the house they were crowding the sea-front cafés for meals of fried fish and chips, or joining the column of people steadily passing through the revolving door of Louis Tussaud's Waxworks. By the time he and Arny had finished lunch, in the same tense silence of breakfast, the rain was a steady downpour. Some of the boarders sat on aimlessly in the dining-room after the meal, but Frank got up as soon as he had finished his sweet and went up to the room. A few minutes later Arny came in.

'Lousy weather,' he muttered.

'Rotten.'

'Not going out this afternoon?'

Frank shrugged. 'Nowhere to go.' He sat on the upright chair by the window and fingered the crease in one leg of his trousers. They would have found somewhere to go. A drop of rain would not have kept them in – before . . .

Arny took off his jacket and hung it in the wardrobe.

'What did you do this morning?'

'Sat on the pier for a while.'

All at once he was certain that Arny knew every move he had made before lunch; that he had followed him from the moment he left the house.

'Are you seeing the girlfriend again?'

'I've got to phone her.'

'Did you see a paper this morning?'

'Yes.'

'The one with the description?'

'What description?' Frank said. His heart had quickened. He looked up to meet Arny's thin, contemptuous smile.

' "The police wish to interview a man of medium height wearing a fawn mackintosh and trilby hat who was seen in the vicinity of the shop about the time of the robbery." In other words, they don't know a thing.'

'I wouldn't be too sure.'

'What d'you mean?'

'Those chaps are clever. And they don't tell the papers everything.'

'They're only clever if they've got something to work on.'

He watched Frank, who was smoking now as he looked at the curtain of rain outside. In a moment he said, 'What about coming in with me, Frank? You wouldn't say no to a hundred quid, would you?'

'I would to that hundred.'

'I could take you back to the Smoke with me as well; introduce you to some people, put you on the trail of some real money instead of what you earn in that office.' When Frank did not answer but gave a little disbelieving shake of his head, Arny went on, 'But I doubt if you've got the guts for it.'

'Don't you mean "stomach"?'

'Either way. Look, Frank, you remember how it was when we were kids. We were in that together, weren't we? The two of us.'

Frank turned his head. 'For God's sake, Arny, don't you know the difference between that and this?'

Arny came and sat on the edge of Frank's bed. 'It's the old man that's bothering you, isn't it? I didn't mean to hit him, y'know. I give you my word.'

'What was the gun for?'

'To frighten him.'

'Where do you get things like that?'

'Plenty of stuff kicking about since the war, if you know where to ask.'

106

'And you know, don't you? What kind of business are you in down there? What kind of people are you mixed up with?'

'I'm mixed up with people who'll lead me to the pot of gold, old son.'

'And how many more old men will that mean you've got to knock on the head?'

'Cool it, Frank, cool it. I'm tired of talking to you.'

'Then don't,' Frank said.

Arny got up off the bed and took a pair of shoes out of the wardrobe. He had brought a small leather case containing polish, a brush and a duster. He sat on his own bed and began to put a shine on a shine while Frank lit another cigarette and watched the rain streaming down the window. Frank wondered who would stick it longest; who would be driven into the rain first.

Chapter Thirty-four

The rain streamed also down the window of the rear ground-floor bedroom of Mr and Mrs Truscott where Truscott, his huge abused body sprawled diagonally across the double bed, under the crumpled and disordered sheets, was just waking from fourteen hours of drunken sleep. He had been dreaming and his mind was a well of shadowy erotic images as he came awake and stirred sluggishly and opened his eyes.

Turning over, he saw the rain-misted window as he raised his eyes from the clock and realised that he had missed the lunchtime opening of the pubs. He groped back into his mind for the pictures that had been so clear a little while ago. It had been a lovely dream. He had had Brenda just where he wanted her and she had been only too willing and ready. He moved his legs under the sheet, his body slack with drowsy desire. If only Brenda were here beside him now. The weather could please itself then. It could rain for a fortnight if it wanted to. Brenda, Brenda . . . she was a living torment . . .

Truscott had been a fine enough man at one time, and he himself seemed sometimes to realise the waste of his life. Occasionally, when maudlin with drink, he would corner some stranger and ramble self-pityingly back over the wasted years to the time when he had been a mighty man with the blacksmith's hammer, respected in his job, courting Ginny, his only small vices an occasional flutter on a horse, a few shillings a week on a football pool and a fondness for a drink on his way home from work. He had deserved a drink in those days: he

108

worked hard. It was a hard job, one that only a few special men could stick for long. And he had done it all his working days, starting as a nipper out of school, making tea for the men, who drank gallons of it to replace the juices sucked out of them by the hellish heat of the furnaces. There had been a pride, a satisfaction that he had found nowhere since. Steady days: his job, the drink on the way home, courting Ginny. But all that was gone now. Now he could drink when he liked. Now he no longer needed the job. Now he no longer wanted his wife.

He had missed the pub. And he had not eaten for nearly twenty-four fours. He threw back the bed-clothes and put his feet to the floor. When he stood up he groaned. He had slept far too long: he was thickheaded with the surfeit of sleep. He stretched himself in his yesterday's crumpled shirt and crossed barefoot to the basin where he swilled his head and face with cold water. He felt a little better. He pulled on his trousers and fastened his belt. Pushing his bare feet into laceless plimsolls, he left the room in search of food.

Chapter Thirty-five

Brenda sat in an easy chair in the kitchen, her feet up on the fireplace, smoking a cigarette and reading a magazine of so-called true love stories. She was alone. Mrs Truscott had gone off in a taxi straight after lunch to visit a sick friend at Bispham and would not be back until time to prepare tea. It was not often that her aunt left Brenda to carry on alone but whenever she did Brenda resented it. Now she lingered in her comfortable chair, postponing the time when she would have to tackle the mountain of dirty luncheon dishes. The very thought of them put her in a bad temper.

Blackpool had deceived Brenda. It had seemed to her to offer an escape from the grim, cobbled boredom of her home town to a world of holiday lights and gaiety. She had imagined herself hostess to different bright and charming people every week and in her free time consorting with worldly men with money to burn. She must have been out of her mind. Why had she not known that she would be little more than a scullery maid and waitress to an endless dreary stream of people who were precisely the kind she had thought to leave behind? The men she met were mostly those who considered a couple of drinks adequate payment for the liberties they invariably tried to take. Not that they weren't some of them good fun; but they were not the kind a girl could hang on to and climb with. They were small-time, interested only in the bolstering drink and the quick casual conquest. But now there was Arny . . .

She twisted her head as she heard someone's heavy creaking approach on the stairs.

She knew at once who it was. She had hoped, with Ginny out, that he would sleep all afternoon. Without looking at him, which she never did in the normal way of things, she thought how much she loathed him: his sloppy body, his piggy eyes, his thin, lifeless hair, his drinking. Most of all she loathed him for the way he felt about her.

He paused at the foot of the stairs and took in her and the room while he scratched his ribs through the soiled shirt.

'Where's Ginny?'

'Nipped out for five minutes.' She dared not tell him that Ginny would be gone for a couple of hours.

'Is there no dinner?'

'You've missed it; been over long since.'

Her aunt had left instructions that he was to be given sandwiches if he asked. But Brenda was not going to offer anything until he did ask.

He moved into the room, scratching vacantly. Without turning her head again Brenda kept an eye on the distance between them.

'What is there, then?' he asked finally.

'Cold beef sandwich,' Brenda said, not stirring.

'Aye, all right.' He reached up and took a cigarette from a packet on the mantelshelf and lit it with a match.

'Here,' Brenda said, 'them's my cigs!'

'Shouldn't leave 'em lying about,' Truscott said, coughing as he drew down the smoke. 'Anyway, you don't begrudge your uncle a cig, surely.'

'Shan't have to, shall I?'

Carefully, deliberately Brenda finished the piece she was reading before getting up to make Truscott's sandwiches.

He watched her craftily as she moved about the room. It excited him even to be alone with her. She had on a green overall, worn and shrunken with washing. He guessed she wore little under it and the movement of her body inside it turned his innards liquid.

Brenda cut several slices of the beef before she

111

realised there was no bread out. She crossed the room and went into the back larder. Turning to come out with several loaves in her arms she found the doorway blocked by Truscott.

He had startled her and she spoke more shrilly than she intended. 'What d'you want?'

'Summat to wash me sandwiches down with.'

'You want to stop creepin' about after folk, scaring 'em out of their wits.'

'There's a crate of beer down by your legs,' Truscott said. He made no move to come nearer, but barred the doorway, his eyes on her, big hands slack at his sides, like bunches of pink uncooked sausages.

She fancied she saw the hands twitch as though preparing to reach for her and her heart suddenly hammered with real fear.

'Get it yourself,' she said. 'My hands are full.'

She stood aside, drawing back as he came to pass her. Another second and her way would be clear. But he stopped and put one hand on her shoulder.

'What's there to be scared of, Brenda? There's only you and me.'

She felt the pulsing lecherous heat of his hand through her overall and tried to shrug it off.

'Gerraway, you daft brush.'

'I can look after you, y'know,' Truscott said. 'A fiver a week's nothing to me. You can have it. You can have it willingly if only you'll be nice to me. Just now and again, y'understand. Only now and again. Think what you could do with another fiver a week. And there's nobody else need know.'

The slobbering pleading in his voice sickened her and she tried to push by.

'That's enough of that. I don't want your money. God knows what Ginny would say if she knew what you were up to.'

'Ginny,' Truscott hissed, 'What's Ginny got to do with you an' me?'

With a sudden movement he had knocked the loaves

out of her arms and was embracing her in a bear-like hug.

'Give us a kiss, Brenda love. Just a little kiss.'

As she felt the bad breath of regurgitated beer on her face she yelled at him, 'Gerroff. Gerroff, you dirty old sod,' and hacked at his ankle.

He shifted his leg and she felt him off-balance. She threw the weight of her body sideways and they fell together, sprawling over a box and on to a pile of sacks. His full weight settled on to her, crushing her into the sacks. His loose lips trailed saliva across her face and as they poised above her mouth she twisted her head, hysteria rising in her. He let go of her with one arm and a button shot across the larder as he tore open the front of her overall and thrust his hand to the flesh inside. Her right hand freed, Brenda clawed down with all her strength. Truscott screamed as the five pointed nails lifted the flesh of his cheek.

He was suddenly a dead weight on top of her and she rolled him aside and lurched to her feet. She left everything and ran for the stairs, not stopping till she reached the hall where, seeing it empty, she halted for a moment to ease her pounding heart and suck the aching fingertips of her right hand. Then fear of pursuit drove her on again, staggering and running and falling, up the three flights of stairs into the top of the house and the refuge of her own room.

There she slammed the door and bolted it and threw herself across the bed, clutching the pillows as her entire body was caught in an uncontrollable spasm of revulsion and fear. She thought she would never hold herself still again.

113

Chapter Thirty-six

She was only dimly aware of the knock which came on her door a few moments later. Then as she heard the doorknob turn and the knock repeated, light but insistent, she raised her head, every nerve stretched at the thought of Truscott and the violence he would surely inflict on her if he got near. Almost at once, though, she realised that he could not have hauled his bulk up all those stairs so soon after her.

'Who is it?'

The low voice answered, 'Arny.'

She got up and opened the door. Arny stepped in and closed it behind him, taking in her appearance as she walked away round the bed.

'I saw you come up the stairs,' he said, 'as though Jack the Ripper was behind you.'

She ran her fingers through her short hair and examined her overall where the button was missing.

'You're all worked up,' Arny said.

Her hands trembled. Her mouth quivered. The hysteria had subsided but she was still close to tears.

'What the hell's been going on?' Arny said.

'Ginny's husband,' Brenda said. 'He got me by meself downstairs.'

Arny's eyes widened a fraction. 'You mean he's got a lech for you?'

She sat on the bed and twisted her handkerchief in her fingers. 'He's tried it on before, but he's never been that close.' She trembled as though she was losing control again.

Arny sat down beside her. 'Steady on. Take it easy. The main thing is you got away. You did, didn't you?'

'And I left him something to remember me by.' Brenda looked at the fingernails of her right hand. They still ached. 'I don't feel safe any more, though. I thought I could take care of him but he'll be wild now. He'll have it in for me now. There's no telling what he might do. One night he'll creep up here while I'm asleep.' She was driving herself into hysteria again now with visions of the revenge Truscott might seek, and her hands worked furiously on the limp square of handkerchief.

Arny put his hand over hers and stopped their movement.

'Easy does it.'

'I shall have to get out of here,' she said. 'I can't stop here now.'

Arny slipped his arm round her waist. He could hardly see in this trembling, demoralised girl the brazen, worldly Brenda of yesterday.

'As long as you don't do a bunk before the end of the week,' he said.

'Oh, you,' she said, 'you never take anything serious.'

'Oh, every now and again I do,' Arny said. 'But what's the point in getting all het up about this? You surprise me. I thought you were tougher than that. Don't tell me nobody ever tried it on before.'

'Some people can't bear snakes,' Brenda said. 'That's the way I am with him. I could scream when he comes within a yard of me.'

Arny pushed her gently back across the bed and put his mouth to her neck. 'You're not like that with me, though, are you?'

'You know I'm not.'

'Tell me what you feel like then,' he said.

'Like I don't give a damn about anything or anybody. Only what . . . what we're doing together.'

'That's how it should be,' Arny said. 'It's the only way to live.'

115

But when he went to her mouth she put her fingers against his lips.

'Please, Arny; not just now. Later, eh?'

'Okay.'

'It's just that I can still feel him at me.'

'Well, I don't have to rape you in the cellar. I've had you, remember? Remember? Forget him and think about that.'

'I will. Keep your arms round me. I feel safe like that.'

He felt the shudder in her. 'Jesus! He did give you a turn. What did you do to him?'

'Clawed my fingernails across his face. They still hurt.'

Arny took her hand and kissed her fingers before drawing her nails down his cheek. Brenda frowned and straightened her fingers and stroked his face with the inside of her hand. Adjusting his weight, Arny slipped his free hand into her overall and lightly held one taut breast.

'Arny . . .'

'Hmmm?'

'Do you like me?'

'Whatever gave you that idea?'

'Go on, be serious.'

'You know I think you're great.'

'I'm crazy about you, Arny. Funny, isn't it? In two days. You know there's been other fellers, but none of 'em were like you.'

Arny frowned, his face in her neck. He felt suddenly uneasy at where all this might be leading.

'We've had some marvellous times, love; and we'll have a few more yet.'

'I don't like to think of you going away on Saturday.'

'Yeh, a pity I didn't fix up for a fortnight.'

'Can't you stop another week?'

' 'Fraid not. Got to get back to the job Monday.'

'Didn't you say you were your own boss?'

'I've got a partner. Can't leave it all to him, or he might get to thinking he can do as he likes. Besides, somebody else will be wanting the room.'

116

'Plenty of people could fit in a single man.'

'Sure, there's room for me here.'

'Where?'

'Right where I am this minute.'

'Don't think I wouldn't, either,' Brenda said, 'if I thought there wouldn't be any talk. But Ginny 'ud find you somewhere.'

'Yeh, well it's a shame, but I've got to be back in the Smoke next week.'

'The Smoke?'

'London Town.'

'Have you got a fag?'

'Sure.'

He sat up and lit cigarettes for both of them. Brenda drew deeply.

'I feel a lot better now. God knows what I'll tell Ginny, though, when she comes in and finds the pots still waiting to be washed.'

'Might be as well not to tell her about old slobber-guts. She might think you've been giving him the come-on.'

'If she'll think that she'll think anything.'

'I don't know . . . Just play it canny.'

'Arny . . . What's London like?'

'London? You mean you've never been there?'

'No. I've seen it on the pictures any number of times, but I've never been.'

'Well, it's big, that's the first thing. Enormous. And it's exciting. You feel anything could happen. Anywhere else, you're on the edge of things, but in London you're bang in the middle, where everything happens. There's no place like it.'

He glanced sideways at her profile as she sat slightly hunched on the edge of the bed. All that cockiness and she had never even been to London. She was just a poor green provincial floozie. He had got up to get an ash tray from the dressing-table when she spoke next:

'Arny, will you take me with you?'

'Take you?'

'To London.'

'On a trip, you mean? To show you round? I can fix that later, if you want. Come in winter, when the season's over here.'

'I mean to stay, to live there.'

'It's not as bad as all that here, is it?'

'I've got to get away from here. Don't you want to take me?'

'Don't get me wrong, love. There's all kinds of things to consider.' He had not foreseen this. He had his life, she had hers. Why couldn't they have a bit of fun and call it a day? 'Where would you live? What would you do?'

'You said I could model.'

'And you could, once you broke in. But you'd need money and a place to live while you did the rounds.'

'I could get a job as a waitress easy enough.' She ran her forefinger up and down between the tendons on the back of his hand. 'And I could live with you. I'd be your girlfriend. Nobody 'ud talk in London, would they? I'd be your mistress. I wouldn't care who knew there. Haven't I been a good mistress to you this last two days?'

'I'll say,' Arny said. 'But y'see, I don't live alone. I share this place with Jackie and there just isn't room for anybody else.'

'We could find another place.'

'Easier said than done, love. Besides, I'm under a kind of obligation to the bloke. It's hard to explain, but he let me bunk in with him when I first hit town. He likes my company and he'd, well, he'd be miffed if I moved out just now. I don't want to cross him. He's the senior partner. He started the business.'

It was not much of a story. He could have done much better with a bit of notice. Imagine his landlady if he tried to bring a dame in to live with him. Imagine Brenda seeing him as Norrie's part-time errand boy after the tale he had spun her. She was a marvellous screw – well, no she wasn't if the truth was told: she had the kind of body that made you think she would be and could make you forget she wasn't. For a while. But he'd be screaming in a fortnight. No, where he was going it was

118

better to travel alone. Until he made it and could pick and choose.

He was about to say he would write to her, keep in touch, when she spoke abruptly.

'You don't want to take me.'

He fondled her. 'No, it's not that.'

'It's just that.' She pushed him away and sprang up off the bed.

Arny got up too. He stubbed out his cigarette and stood under the dormer window, looking at the brightening sky, his hands pushed deep into his trousers' pockets.

'If you're really set on going why not go on your own and I'll see you there?'

'I wanted to go with you. I thought after the way we'd been together you might think a bit about me. But it'll be ta-ra without another thought once this week's over.'

Arny was losing interest rapidly.

'You're building a lot on two days.'

'It was just a bit of fun to you, wasn't it?'

'Why not?' Arny shrugged. 'I can't see why you want to leave here at all. Not just now, anyway. Here's old man Truscott with his pockets full of readies and all a-dither for you. Why don't you teach yourself to be nice to him and put a little nest-egg together before you leave?'

Standing with his back to her he did not see the first flush of genuine anger in her face.

'What do you mean?'

'Mean?' Arny turned but barely glanced at her. 'I mean you're a sight better off here emptying his pockets than washing pots in London.'

'What do you take me for?' she said, and the shrill lift of her voice made him raise his eyes and look directly at her. 'Do you think I open my legs for any man when I've known him twenty-four hours?'

'Of course I don't,' Arny said insolently, 'but Truscott's in the family, isn't he?'

Brenda's eyes glittered with outrage. So she had been

119

easy from time to time, but she had always done it to please and never purely for gain. After what she had told Arny about Truscott and he had seen the state she was in, she could hardly believe what he was suggesting.

'I'd like to know what the bloody hell you think I am.'

All at once Arny was sick of it, of her, of the whole affair. Pillaging the world for his pleasure, he lived by no rule except the bidding of his desire. Now he was in danger of becoming involved, and with this one of all people, this cheap little Lancashire slut with her scrubby overall, her bottled hairdo and the sordid room which stank of her fear.

'Now what do *you* think I think you are?' he retorted, his voice as deliberate as the gaze he ran slowly over the whole of her, insolently, with a sarcastic contempt in his eyes that made her face flame.

'Well I know what *you* are!' she burst out. The words on her tongue were 'cosh-boy' and 'thief'. But some last controlling instinct made her swallow them. 'You're one of them,' she modified lamely, ' 'at wants his pleasures without paying for 'em.'

Arny's lips tightened. 'Now why didn't you say so?' His right hand came free of his pocket and he walked across to the door as he peeled one-pound notes from the roll. He dropped a couple on the bed then added a third. 'I think that's fair enough,' he said. 'You can't expect to command professional rates, can you?'

Chapter Thirty-seven

He was sorry before he had taken half a dozen steps outside her room. Not for having humiliated her, but because he had cut off that source of pleasure for the rest of the holiday. Tonight, when he had calmed down, he would be ready to share her bed again, and now that was lost to him. He had handled it very badly. Always he underestimated their pride. He said aloud, 'Oh, shit! Shit! Shit! Shit!' as he went down the stairs.

Frank looked up as he entered the room. He saw at once that Arny was wild.

'Women! Christ!' Arny scuffed savagely at the edge of the carpet. 'Old Truscott tried to rape her down in the basement. Now she's got the wind up. Wants me to take her to London with me. Or she did. We've had a row. I reckon that's the last of Brenda as far as I'm concerned. Oh, blast it, what's this holiday coming to?' He met Frank's gaze. 'You're okay, anyway. You've still got your little copper's niece in tow, haven't you?'

'Is that all you can think about, Arny?'

'What else should I be thinking about, eh? I suppose I should be searching my conscience and plucking up enough courage to go and tell the cops I've been a naughty boy, but I'll do my best to mend my ways during the five years they've got me in stir!'

He came closer and bent to look at Frank, biting off his words with savage deliberation.

'Well, get this straight, mate. I'm not doing time for you or anybody else. I was in a jam. I needed money. So I planned a way to get it. It took guts, chum, more guts

121

than you'll ever have; and it came off. Only two little things went wrong: I had to hit the old boy, and I lost my wallet. But the wallet's getting them nowhere, and as for the old man – okay, I'm sorry I hit him, but he's had his life and mine's just beginning. And how I'm going to make it crack!'

He took his jacket off its hanger. 'It's stopped raining. I'm going out for a breath of air.'

He glanced back at Frank as he opened the door. But Frank had already turned away for fear that Arny might read his face.

Chapter Thirty-eight

At tea, which was later than usual for some reason unknown to any of the boarders except Frank and Arny, there was an envelope on Arny's plate. He sat down and tore it open. Inside were three one-pound notes and a letter from Brenda. It said, 'I am sorry I was so silly but you will know how upset I was and I know it was me being silly made you mad. I know you did not mean it and I didn't either. Hoping we can still be friends. If so I have an errand to run on the South Shore tonight and can meet you by the Big Dipper on the Pleasure Beach about half-nine. Just nod if you will be there.'

Arny raised his eyebrows and put the note and the money in his pocket. 'She's got more sense than I gave her credit for,' he said across the table to Frank, who guessed what had happened when Brenda brought their tea-pot and Arny looked up at her and nodded. 'Message received. Wilco.'

There was a faint suffusion of colour under her thick make-up. She did not meet his eyes but nodded in return and said, 'Yes. All right.'

Chapter Thirty-nine

Frank met Rona off a bus by the Winter Gardens in the early evening and steered her into the nearest presentable-looking pub. They found a corner in a three-quarters empty lounge bar.

'What can I get you?'

'Unless you're thinking of making a night of it I can manage a gin and tonic.'

He came back to her a moment or two later, leaving her gin and his Scotch on the bar.

'I haven't any money.'

Rona started to open her handbag as the irony of the situation struck Frank with force and he said 'God!' with such bitter emphasis that she looked up at him in question.

'A ten-shilling note do?'

'That's plenty.'

'You haven't lost it, have you?'

'No, I know exactly where it is. I changed my jacket.'

As he went back to the bar counter he could see Arny in his mind's eye, patting his pockets in that other, crowded pub, the innocent victim of a petty theft. Forty-eight hours ago, before the world changed.

'You're still only half with me, aren't you?' Rona said, when he had brought the drinks.

'I'm sorry.'

'You didn't *have* to bring me out tonight. I'd have kept on a low light for a while.'

Once I've told her, he was thinking, there'll be no taking it back. *If* I tell her.

'Have you ever gone through a time in your life,' he asked her, 'when you relied on someone else, almost completely, and they were the measure of everything?'

'Are you talking about your cousin again?'

He nodded, taking out cigarettes and offering them.

'My parents were killed within about four months of each other: my father in the retreat to Dunkirk, my mother in a car crash. There was a man with her. She'd been seeing men all the time my father was away. I wasn't old enough to understand in detail all that involved, but I knew that she'd put herself beyond the pale and people talked about her. When older women looked at me in the street I thought they were wondering when the bad blood would come out.

'Arny saved me then. I quite simply don't know what I'd have done if he'd not been there. He tried to drill into me a sense of my own identity; the kind of sense he had of himself. He was Arny and nobody else. Take him or leave him. I was Frank. Who were these people to throw their sidelong looks and judge me for what my mother had been? He made me his friend, confidant, accomplice. I warmed myself in his sun.

'All that lasted pretty much until Arny went to do National Service. For over a year, until my turn came, I was on my own with Uncle Vernon and Aunt Carrie; and by the time I had to leave myself I knew I'd never be coming back to them.

'I suppose I still harbour guilt over Aunt Carrie. Try as I might, I could never get fond of her. She had too much bitterness and gall in her for any really loving relationship. Religion made Uncle Vernon want to open his arms to all men; with Aunt Carrie it was a turn of the shoulder and a whispered "Holier than thou!" '

'You've never said what your uncle does.'

'He's a jobbing carpenter.'

'How appropriate.'

'Oh, yes. And he knows it. Well, while Arny was there to keep it in proportion you'd somebody to laugh about it with. It was after he went that it got out of hand. She

125

turned her resentment on me, as if something about me provided a channel for all the bitterness in her. It goes without saying that she'd never had any time for my mother, and now she began to look for signs of her in me. If you want to find things like that, you will.

'My leaves rarely coincided with Arny's but we exchanged a letter or two and as soon as I realised he'd no intention of settling at home again I began to make my own decisions.'

'Why didn't you go to London as well?'

'I don't know. Something held me. Unfinished business. If I'd gone straight off it would somehow have seemed like running away.' He shrugged and frowned. He had never explained that satisfactorily to himself. 'I knew I'd clear out one day,' he said. 'I was just waiting for the sign that said it was the right time.'

'So you never resumed your friendship – you and Arny?'

'Not on the old terms, no. You change. You grow up. Grow apart.'

'But old affections go deep, don't they? Old loyalties . . .'

Loyalties. Yes.

'And I see now that this holiday is something of a reunion.'

'Yes, something like that.'

'And I guess that somehow it's not quite working out.'

'Do you?'

'Is it because I'm taking up all your time?'

'I wouldn't let you if I didn't want you to.'

'Wouldn't you?'

'No.'

What right had he to inflict on her something she would surely have chosen not to know: to inflict that knowledge on her because he could not bear its burden alone?

That pawnshop robbery in Cressley that your uncle was talking about, he would say.

There was something about it in the papers, wasn't there?

That's all it was to her – something in the papers that her uncle had gossiped about.

I know who did it.

And her mind making the connecting leap and drawing back, appalled. Oh, no, surely . . .

He had no right. He couldn't anyway. Old Loyalties . . . Even though Arny didn't give tuppence for the old man. Even though all he was bothered about was getting away with it. Even though he hadn't finished: this was just for starters and there was no telling what might be next. Even though Arny had turned into a criminal. Do what you like, take what you want. Who gives a fuck for the stupid good people? What do they know?

Shouldn't they at least be warned not to put their trust in the likes of Arny Whitmore? Wasn't it his, Frank's, duty to warn them; because he was the only one who knew?

He found himself on his feet. She was looking up at him.

'Come on, let's get some air.'

'Where are we going?'

'First we'll go back to the digs and get my money. It's not far, but if you'd like me to meet you somewhere . . .'

'I'll go with you.'

'Okay.'

'I don't know why, but my instinct tells me not to let you out of my sight.'

She took his arm as they went through the door.

Chapter Forty

There was a saloon car standing outside the house. It was the only car in the street. At the foot of the steps Frank said, 'Do you want to wait out here or in the hall? I shall only be a minute.'

'I'll come in.'

Frank could hear voices as he crossed the hall. At the sound of the front door closing Mrs Truscott put her head out of the dining-room, saw him and spoke over her shoulder.

'Here's the other one now.'

A man appeared. He moved quickly, putting himself between Frank and the front door. As Frank took in the obvious fact that he did not look like a holiday-maker, the man asked.

'Are you a guest here, sir?'

'Yes.'

'Can I have your name, please.'

Frank told him and the man half-turned to take in Rona.

'Is the young lady with you?'

'Yes.'

'Will you both come this way?'

Brenda and Mrs Truscott were in the dining-room with a big man, who wore what looked like rather a well-cut suit under his raincoat. Frank thought that everybody must surely be able to hear his heart thumping.

Brenda said, 'That's the other one, the cousin, Frank,' and the big man said, 'Is Arny Whitmore your cousin, sir?' Frank nodded. 'We're police officers. We have reason to believe he can help us with our inquiries. Do you happen to know where he is now?'

'No.'

'When did you see him last?'

'At tea-time, here.'

'I've told you where he is,' Brenda said. 'Or where he'll be at half-past nine.'

'Please, Miss Hogan, will you try not to speak until I ask you a question.'

Frank was looking round to try to see Rona when the big man spoke to him.

'You do know what this is all about, don't you?'

Frank swallowed. 'I don't understand.'

'What don't you understand?'

'I heard you,' Brenda said. 'I heard you this morning. You and Arny.'

'I shall have to put you outside, Miss Hogan.'

'Ask him,' Brenda said. 'Ask him what they were talking about.'

'All right, I will.' The big man looked at Frank. 'I'd like you to cast your mind back to a conversation you had with your cousin around six-thirty this morning. And if you say another word till you're spoken to, Miss Hogan, I'll have you locked up where you can talk to yourself.'

'You wouldn't have known anything about it but for me,' Brenda said.

Frank said, 'Does Miss Fairlie have to hear all this? It's got nothing to do with her.'

Rona had moved now into his field of vision.

'What is it all about, Frank?'

'You remember that robbery your uncle was talking about?'

'Oh, that. But—'

'Just a minute,' the big man said. 'This is running away with us. Who is your uncle and what has he to do with it?'

'Len Rogers. He was on the force here.'

'I didn't know you,' the other officer said. 'You're Len Rogers' niece, eh?'

'Yes.'

It suddenly came to Frank that without Rogers' story of the stolen wallet none of this would have happened. He could have heard about the robbery and never for a second connected it with Arny. All of this stemmed from that relish in passing on inside information. And from his, Frank's, meeting Rona. He met Rona's look and could not read what she was thinking.

'You'd better tell us the story from the beginning, Mr Whitmore,' the big man said.

He supposed he had no choice now. None at all.

'Do you want to sit down?'

'I'm all right standing, thanks.'

'Well then, we're ready when you are.'

'You haven't told me who you are,' Frank said.

'I'm Detective Chief Inspector Feather and this is Detective-Sergeant Ransome.' He nodded. 'Please carry on.'

Chapter Forty-one

'Does that fit in with what you heard, Miss Hogan?'
Feather asked Brenda, when Frank had finished.

'Yes. This one was giving the other one a right telling-
off; calling him a bloody fool and I don't know what
else.'

'Of course you had no idea that Miss Hogan knew the
first thing about it,' Feather said to Frank.

'No, I hadn't.'

'As far as you were aware you were the only one who
did know about it.'

'Yes.'

'You've known since early this morning yet you still
hadn't got round to coming to us. What have you been
doing all day?'

'Walking about wondering what to do.'

'You felt you had a choice?'

'Yes, I thought I had a choice. You don't just walk out
and hand your best friend over to the police. I thought I
might get him to give himself up.'

'But you had no success in that direction.'

'No.'

He wondered if they expected him to condemn Arny
out of hand. But what business was it of theirs if
he had suddenly seen all the viciousness in him?
They would get him now. There would be the trial and
the publicity. He, Frank, would have to tell his story
again – and again. Well, he would tell it; but not
by one word or inflection would he add to Arny's
punishment.

131

Feather turned to Brenda. 'And you, Miss Hogan, what held you back so long?'

Brenda flushed. 'I didn't rightly understand at first. And I thought, well it's none of my business. Then I happened to pick up the paper and I sort of put two and two together. Then I was a bit scared. I had to pluck up me courage.'

'You wouldn't give us your name when you telephoned. We had to keep you talking while we traced the call.'

'And I fell for that.'

'Of course you did. You wanted to be sure we had enough information to apprehend this man. What was the use of phoning otherwise, eh?'

'Well, I didn't want to get mixed up in it.'

'You were on friendly terms with this Arnold Whitmore, weren't you?'

'I never laid eyes on him before Saturday.'

'But since then you've become friendly enough to arrange an appointment with him this evening, which enabled you to tell us where and when we could find him.'

'He seemed a nice enough chap at first.'

'Yes. There's one thing I don't quite understand, er, Mr Whitmore. You say your cousin came into your room and surprised you in the act of examining his case . . .'

'Yes.'

'And this was in the early morning, around six-thirty. Where was your cousin at that time, made you think you had an opportunity to look at his things?'

Frank merely shrugged and Feather looked from him to Brenda and back again.

'Perhaps we'll let that pass for the present.'

'You may as well know now as later,' Brenda said in a rush. 'He'd been with me.'

Mrs Truscott clucked with outraged surprise and the inspector said, 'I see,' and rubbed his jaw. 'That explains a couple of points I wasn't clear on. Have you got all that, Sergeant?'

Ransome said, 'Yes, sir.'

'I shall want you all to make proper statements in due course.' The Detective Chief Inspector gazed blandly round the room. He was not looking at any one of them in particular when he said, 'You know, of course, that this is a murder inquiry now?'

Chapter Forty-two

The words, dropped so matter-of-factly into a sudden silence in the room, brought a short sharp squeal from Mrs Truscott. Brenda jerked up her head, fear widening her gaze into a stare. Frank was aware of five pairs of eyes coming to rest on him. He closed his own eyes for a moment. Then he heard himself say, as though he had been directly addressed,

'I didn't know.'

'Perhaps it was released too late for the evening papers,' Feather said. 'I'm sorry if I've upset you.'

You bastard, Frank thought. Of course you've upset me. He gripped the back of a dining-chair as Rona moved round to his side and he felt her hand slip under his arm. Murder . . . Oh, God! Oh, Arny . . .

Feather said, 'Now I think we'd better examine the evidence, if it's still there.'

Oh, Jesus Christ and God Almighty.

'With your permission, madam.'

'I don't suppose it matters tuppence what I say,' Mrs Truscott said. 'I don't know what'll happen to my custom after this. I thought I was running a decent respectable house. I didn't know it was a hideout for murderers, and my own niece turning it into a . . .' She balked at the word. 'First my husband, and now—'

'You say it,' Brenda flared. 'You just say it and I'll have him put where he belongs.'

'What's all this?' Feather asked.

Mrs Truscott bit her lip. Brenda stared hard at her.

134

'Just a bit of domestic trouble, that's all. Nothing at all to do with this.'

'You step this way, Miss Hogan. There's no need for you to come up, Mrs Truscott, if you don't care to.'

'If you want me I'll be down in the kitchen, having a cup of tea.'

'Perhaps you'd take Miss, er, with you. Take her and give her a cup. You don't need to go running off anywhere, do you, Miss, er . . .'

'Fairlie.'

'Miss Fairlie. Do you?'

'No.' Rona shook her head and squeezed Frank's arm. 'I'll be waiting, Frank.'

He put his hand over hers. 'Thanks.'

'We'll let you lead the way, then, Mr Whitmore.'

Chapter Forty-three

Feather passed the roll of banknotes back to his colleague and spun the chamber of the revolver.

'Was it empty this morning?'

'I don't know. I don't know much about guns, and I'd hardly touched it before Arny walked in.'

Ransome had tipped everything out of the case.

'There's nothing else here, sir.'

'Try his clothes.'

The sergeant went through everything in the wardrobe, Frank's clothes as well as Arny's. 'No luck.' When he came upon Frank's wallet, Frank said, 'That's mine.' He took it from Ransome. 'It's what I came back for.'

'Perhaps,' Feather said, 'he found ammunition harder to come by. Perhaps he didn't want any. Just intended the gun as a frightener.'

'I should think that's the most likely,' Frank said.

'Yes. But as it turned out it became a lethal weapon anyway.' He handed the gun to Ransome. 'Take care of it, Derek. We might get a line on it.'

'Are we going to pick him up, sir?'

'The sooner the better, I'd say. Was your date with him a definite arrangement, Miss Hogan?'

'Oh, yes. He'll be there.'

'But well away from here, eh?' Feather remarked. 'We could take him there or wait for him to come back here.'

'We might surprise him into admitting something if we take him outside, sir.'

'Yes. And when Miss Hogan fails to keep her date he

might get windy and make for the woods. He could do that any time, except that he hasn't got the money.'

'If he reads in the late editions that the old man's dead, sir, he might forget the money in his concern for his neck,' Ransome said.

'You're quite right. I think we're going to have to take him in the open.' Feather looked at his watch. 'We've just nice time . . . He's not carrying any weapon that you know of, Mr Whitmore? A knife, perhaps, or a razor?'

'No, he's not that type.'

'Well then, we'd better have a description.'

Frank began in a lifeless voice to recite the details of Arny's appearance. Age, twenty-six. Five-feet ten in height. Good build. Thick black wavy hair, fresh complexion, clean-shaven, blue eyes . . .

'Any distinguishing features? Scars or the like?'

'No.'

'What is he wearing?'

Frank opened the wardrobe and checked Arny's clothes.

'Greeny grey mixture tweed jacket, dark grey flannels.'

'You haven't a photograph of him?'

'Sorry, no.'

'Could be any one of hundreds,' the sergeant said.

'Too true,' Feather said. 'We must be sure. It wouldn't do to get the wrong man. Especially when the right one would probably be looking on . . .'

Frank had a sudden premonition of what was coming next.

Feather said, 'I'm afraid we shall have to ask one of you to come along and identify him. If you could keep your date, Miss Hogan . . .'

'Not me,' Brenda said. 'You can't make me do that.'

All this had become too much for her. She had no taste for savouring her revenge. She had seen it as a short statement spoken anonymously into a telephone, not an involvement with the law as it mustered its forces to apprehend one man – a man with whom she had known

137

the closest of physical intimacy. She was drained of all vindictive feeling towards Arny now: she was, in fact, feeling rather sorry for him, the way his time was running out. Oh, and he had seemed to hold such promise, for a while. Her deliverer. Such a pity. But that was over now. There was no sense in dwelling on it. She was finished with that as she was finished with this house. Somewhere below was Truscott with his cheek under ointment and gauze. Her aunt had blamed her for that. Astonishingly, for Brenda had always thought Ginny to be free of illusions about her husband. So it was back to Oldham for her, and the clatter and hum of the factory, a sound she had thought never to hear again, a sound which now sang to her of comfort and security: dull but safe. And later on, one fine day, who could tell . . .?

'No,' she heard herself say again. 'Not likely.'

There was a silence. 'It'll have to be me, then,' Frank said.

Feather looked at Frank, then nodded. He turned to Ransome.

'All right. Now you, Derek, stay here in case he comes back.' Disappointment showed in Ransome's face. 'I need somebody here, Derek, who knows everything that's happened. I'll send you another man, but keep out of sight. I'll take the car with me. First of all now, go down to the phone and get hold of the Chief. Tell whoever you speak to that it's number-one priority. Try his home number first and tell me as soon as you have him. Take Miss Hogan with you. She stays right by you till this thing's over. The Fairlie girl as well.' As Frank lifted his hand and made as if to speak, Feather said, 'You weren't thinking of taking her along for the ride, were you, Mr Whitmore?'

Frank shook his head. 'No.'

Ransome and Brenda left the room. Feather took a mint out of his pocket and unwrapped it.

'Now, Mr Whitmore. Here's what you'll have to do.'

Chapter Forty-four

Frank and the inspector sat together in the back of the car. Feather was quiet now, picking at a corner of fingernail. The questions were over for the time being. Now was the time for action. He had planned everything so far as he was able; the outcome now depended upon the speed of reaction of his men and on good fortune. Most important of all it rested on the silent, keyed-up, fair-haired young man beside him. Would he be all right? Would he measure up or would he lose his nerve somewhere along the way? He looked out of his eye-corners at Frank's hands as they fidgeted with the creases in his trousers. Those hands had not been still since he and the lad got into the car. He had guts, though, or he would never have offered himself for this job. It was asking a great deal to have him put the finger right on someone so close. Feather had never experienced a conflict of loyalty of that kind. It was worse than finding yourself next to a bent colleague.

The car was drawn in to the kerb along a side street off Watson Road. Not far away were other cars, in radio communication with this one. All they awaited was the signal to move in.

Frank watched people walk in a steady stream past the end of the road. The evening sun made the interior of the car oppressively warm. He wound his window down three or four inches and thought about Arny somewhere in the fairground; perhaps already waiting for Brenda by the Big Dipper. He thought too of Uncle Vernon and Aunt Carrie and what he was going to say to them afterwards. It was going to ruin their lives. It might end Arny's . . . *to be hanged by the neck until you are dead* . . . Oh, God, no, not that. Surely not the extreme penalty. But wasn't murder while committing a felony one of the worst of crimes?

The inspector stopped picking at his nail and looked at his watch. He sighed and felt in his waistcoat pocket and brought out a packet of spearmint chewing-gum. He extracted a tablet and put it in his mouth. Frank took out his cigarettes.

'Is it all right?'

'Carry on.'

He lit a cigarette then thought to offer the packet to the inspector. Feather looked at it in silence for several seconds, his jaws moving on the gum. Then he took a cigarette and accepted a light. 'Don't know what you're doing to me . . .' He drew deeply and exhaled with satisfaction. He wound down his window and tossed out the chewed pellet of gum. 'A filthy habit, that.'

'Do you . . .?' Frank said.

'What?'

'I was wondering if they'd . . .' He stopped again, unable to utter the words.

'What is it?' Feather said.

'Nothing.'

Feather turned his head. 'Look,' he said, 'I know this can't be easy for you, but don't get the idea that nobody realises it.'

He looked at his watch again and asked for the microphone. One of the men in front passed it back and Feather hunched forward on the edge of his seat. 'Move in now and take your places. You know what to do. Most of you should have nothing to do at all. If you should, get it over with as quickly and as quietly as possible. Remember the public, and that this chap won't mind taking a few risks. He probably knows by now that he has nothing to lose.'

Nothing to lose . . . Frank screwed up his eyes. It was a dream. It was surely a dark mad dream . . .

140

As the car started, Feather said, 'Feeling all right?'

Frank opened his eyes and looked straight ahead. 'I'm okay.'

'Just remember everything I told you. It'll be over in a few minutes.'

'I'll be all right.'

They stopped again fifty yards from the Promenade and a second car pulled in behind.

'It's up to you now,' Feather said. 'As soon as you speak to him we'll take him. But remember, don't look round.'

Frank opened the door and stepped on to the pavement. He slammed the door and the sound was echoed twice from the car behind. He began to walk at a steady pace towards the Promenade, weaving in and out of bunches of people and narrowing his eyes as the evening sun dazzled him with light off the sea.

Chapter Forty-five

Arny hugged the stock of the rifle into his shoulder and, with his cheek close to his thumb, watched the endless belt of white-painted metal ducks move past the sights. This would be his first shot. He had suddenly felt a strong urge to shoot while waiting for Brenda and now he savoured the moment. He knew with certainty that when his right forefinger squeezed the trigger one of those ducks would disappear. He had not fired the gun yet, but he knew. It depended upon him.

Pting! and down it went.

He had killed a man. He had not meant to do it. That was why he had never bothered with ammo for the revolver. Just a bluff. Catch him on a job with a loaded gun! But it had all been for nothing. The old man had had to act stupid and he had known the second he hit him that a nice clean job had been turned into a mess. Looking down at the old man lying there like something waiting for the rag and bone man, he had hated him for his stupidity. The avaricious old sod could have handed over the loot and there would have been no bother. He could have tied him up and left him comfortable. But he was greedy. He had always been greedy. He had once cheated Arny out of some wages: done it and looked him straight in the face. So now his greed had got the better of him and led to his undoing. Arny had felt so viciously angry only a couple of times before. Real bad. Like killing. One time was on manoeuvres in Germany when that big fat slob Calloway, who nobody liked much and a few hated, had cocked up a good patrol by sticking out his fat arse for all to see. As it happened, Arny had him in his sights at the time and got some relief by pulling the trigger and knowing that had they been in a real engagement and using live ammo he wouldn't have been able to stop himself dropping the bastard. The other time was at school when he'd had his hands round Bellis's scrawny neck and was squeezing, squeezing till Tetley, a prefect, pulled him off. Only just in time . . .

Oh, the whole stupid crew of them. The stupid ones and the good ones and those that were both. How he hated all stupid, foolish, good people.

'Are you going to shoot again, then, or are you just resting your elbows?'

They moved past his sights with all the stupid goodness in the world on their smug pudding faces and he squeezed the trigger with murderous deliberation. Pting! again – Pting! again – Pting! Pting! and Pting! Five more down.

He straightened up and looked at the man behind the counter. 'What do I get for that, then?'

The man shrugged. 'Satisfaction?' The nod of his head indicated a small notice on the wall: 'For amusement only.'

Arny said 'Aagh!' in disgust and turned away. Another man slipped into his place and took up the rifle he had used.

He read the report of the old man's death in the evening paper once again as the crowd flowed by over the tarmac. He felt safe here. Safest in a crowd. Hell! Safe anywhere. Right in the cop-shop itself. They hadn't a clue who they were looking for. The town was bulging with visitors. He might be tall or short, fat or thin. He might have a wooden leg and a squint. 'A man of medium height, wearing a raincoat and a trilby hat.' That was a good one! No, there was only Frank, and he would never give him away. He had done a lot for Frank at one time and Frank would never forget it. A big believer in friendship and loyalty, Frank. Now the old man was dead there was even less likelihood of Frank's forgetting all that, because he'd know what they would do to him. No, beyond wringing his hands and moaning about conscience he would do nothing. If it came right down to it, he hadn't the guts.

Oh, these stupid, gutless, decent people with their yap about love and honour and duty, and all the other things that had never meant a thing since the beginning of the world except when some smart guy was using them for his own ends.

He glanced at his watch and looked down through the flow of people to the Big Dipper. It was nearly half-past and she had not arrived. He would not go down there to wait for her: that was not his way. No, once he saw her there he would hang on here for a couple of minutes and then go to her. He wondered why she had chosen this particular place for meeting. Maybe she wanted him to spend some money, to give her a good time. He didn't mind, so long as she paid him back in her own way. But he did not like women to keep him hanging about. He would wait a bit longer, but not too long.

He moved to the next stall, a shooting-gallery also, but with paper targets, and prizes.

'Three shots a tanner! All the best prizes. Win a dolly for your little girl, sir? Only the best prizes. Three shots a tanner.'

Arny put a coin on the counter and was handed a loaded rifle. He took his position on his elbows and looked along the sights. He fired once to see which way the gun threw, then twice more in rapid succession. He paid again, then again, his score mounting. After his last three shots he wound in the target-holder himself. The attendant came up and extracted the square of card, glancing at the jagged-edged hole in the black centre-circle.

'Hard lines, sir.'

'How d'you mean "hard lines"?' Arny said. 'There's three slugs there, straight through the bull.'

'Only one there, sir.'

In a flash of temper Arny slapped down another coin

and demanded three more shots. 'And watch this time.'
The man pushed towards him another rifle, already
loaded, but Arny turned it aside. 'No – load this one
again.'

The man reloaded the gun and inserted a new target.
He wound it back along the wires. Arny fired again.

'Right, wind it in.' They looked together at the three
distinct holes in the bullseye. 'All right?' Arny said.

'Very good shooting, sir,' said the attendant,
unabashed. 'Pick your prize from anywhere on the bottom row, or you can carry on and shoot for a star prize.'

But Arny had lost interest. It was all junk. He pointed
to a small green plaster statuette of a naked girl. 'The bit
in green'll do.' She looked, he thought, rather like
Brenda after Old Man Truscott had been at her.

And where the hell *was* Brenda? Probably run into
some pals and stopped to tell the tale. She'd have plenty
to talk about if she told them all that had happened since
Saturday, without even mentioning Truscott's merry
capers. Or could she just be standing him up, getting her
own back for this afternoon? Take her to London! Take
her to bed for the rest of the week then back to the
Smoke and forget her. Now some of the dames there . . .
He was imagining the look on Norrie's bird's face when
he walked in and dropped the dough in Norrie's lap. Just
casual like, it would be, the way he did it, as though he
could pick up that kind of ready any day of the week.
They'd guess where he'd got it, too, and maybe that
would wipe some of the snot off Angie's face – the reali-
sation, he meant, that he was somebody to be counted.
Not that he intended to make anything of it if she did
soften towards him, though it would be a pleasure to
dally with her any day of the week, otherwise why was
he so keen to impress her? But you had to learn what you
could take and what was better left. And he left that
where it was – in Norrie's keeping. His end away for a
chivving some dark night was no bargain at all.

Now when he got established he'd get himself a real
dame. One with style. He knew the type and it fascinated

him: all fur and scent and icicles. But watch them at a boxing match and see the way their nostrils flared and their eyes filmed over when somebody was getting hurt. It got to him, that did. But it came expensive. The one certain passport was money. He had everything else but that and until it came out of short supply you made do with the Brendas of this world. And if he was being fair, they weren't too bad a substitute and good enough to be going on with. When they turned up, that was . . .

Arny stood with his back to the stall, watching people file through the Big Dipper turnstile. He held the statuette by its head and gently slapped the base into his left palm.

Chapter Forty-six

A few steps inside the gate, and stopping. Oh God, he'd never bargained for this. Sick in his head, as though he had been chain-smoking in a cinema all day; stomach a bottomless pit of fear into which he felt he might fall and be swallowed. Be swallowed by yourself, like the hooley-gooley bird that flew in ever-diminishing circles until it disappeared up its own arsehole.

Two pairs of eyes boring into his back . . . waiting . . . Move, go on, it's twenty-nine minutes past nine. On, then, into the milling, jostling crowd; faces, all with problems behind the expressions. Expressions sober and animated, glum and hilarious; but don't let them fool you, they've all got problems. Any like his? On among white sun-flushed buildings; the Ferris Wheel lifting gently swaying carriages up among the gulls and the white trestle structures of scenic railways: Grand National, Roller Coaster, Big Dipper. Noise surging like a flood: the steel-to-steel roar of the Whip, the screams of girls trapped in the stomach-heaving twist and turn and swoop of the Dive Bomber; and music in a cacophonous amplified roar on all sides.

'Why, Frank! Frank Whitmore!'

The voice snatched him back from somewhere to stare without recognition at the woman's round, bespectacled middled-aged face.

'It is Frank, isn't it?'

'Yes.'

'I was sure it was. I told you it was, George. Well, isn't this a surprise?' The man nodding and speaking

147

normality past the placid briar stem. 'Hullo, Frank.'

'But I don't think he remembers us, George. It's Mr and Mrs Ramsden, Frank; Harker Street. Remember now?'

'Oh, yes, of course.' Why had they slipped so totally without trace from his memory?

'I was only saying to Mr Ramsden the other day that it's such a long time since we saw any of the old Cressley faces, and here we bump into you. How are your aunt and uncle keeping? Well, I hope.'

'Oh, fine.'

'Is your uncle still preaching from time to time? Such a good speaker. What a fine man. I always did like Vernon Whitmore. Well, fancy running into you after all these years. 'Course, Blackpool's the place for that kind of thing, isn't it? Never know who you'll bump into. And what a fine young man you've grown into. How's your cousin Arnold keeping?'

'Oh, grand, fine.' Wonderful, Mrs Ramsden. They'll be hanging him towards the back end of the year. Unless . . . You'll read about it in the papers and you'll tell everybody Why, I was talking to Frank Whitmore that very evening . . .

'And of course he'll have grown too. I don't suppose I'd know him. Has he changed much?'

'No.' A safe answer, Mrs Ramsden. The real one is something I can't give you: has he changed or was he always like this?

'Always such a pleasant boy. Do you remember, George? Always such nice manners.' The time nine-thirty-one and the endless reel of her talk holding him like a chain. 'Are you still living with your uncle and aunt?'

'No, I'm on my own now.'

Would he walk away and leave her standing? Would Arny wait past nine-thirty? Would he leave, this woman's chatter having given him a few hours more? I couldn't help it; she kept me. He's gone. Too bad. I'm out of it. But he won't know what's happened, because I can't tell him.

'Still in Cressley, though? Not married yet? Plenty of time. Doesn't do to rush these things.'

Standing, mesmerised, feet glued to tarmac, listening to advice on marriage.

'But I see you're looking at your watch. You young people, always rushing to places and doing things . . .'

Half-turned the way he had come, looking for two plainclothes men. Nothing but their imagined curses.

'No place like Blackpool, we always say – and we've tried most of the others. Always so much going on. And the air, it's so *enervating*.'

'I really must . . .'

'That's all right. We quite understand. Remember us to all in Cressley, mind.'

'I'll do that.'

'And we shall have to be paying a visit. We really shall.'

Backing away – 'Goodbye, goodbye' – and seeing two purposeful men detach themselves from separate knots of people and come nearer.

Turning, walking on. A queue for bumping boats to carry them into the dreamland grottoes of the River Caves. It's all a dream . . . a dream . . . a nightmare . . . Let me wake up. O God, if there is a God and there can't be, do something, anything. The old man raised from the dead. Better still, it's Saturday morning again and Arny walks past the end of Pym Street without a sideways glance.

He was in sight of the Big Dipper now. Cars were emptying and filling again, people filing down from platform to tarmac, some white-faced, shaken, some laughing. But no Arny. He stopped and stood and looked. There was no Arny. And that was good.

Careful now. Don't panic. Walk nice and slowly to where he can see you. Then stand. Still. So he'll know.

Because there he is, along by those stalls. What's that in his hand? Something he's won. Look this way, Arny. But don't move. Don't react in any way until you've seen me shake my head. Then freeze. Then melt away.

He's looking. He's seen me. He lifts his hand. He lifts his hand and *waves* before the penny drops. Three

149

seconds more and he's got it. He knows and he's running
– *towards me!*

'Fuck you, Frank!' The statuette swings in a green
blur. Into his face. His head snaps back on his neck. He's
down.

A man's shout. A police whistle. Feet padding by.

Chapter Forty-seven

He'd been out. Strong hands sat him up. His left eye was full of blood. A handkerchief flicked from his own breast pocket. 'Here, hold this to it.'

'Where is he?'

'It's all right. He won't get far.'

Struggling to his feet, seeing the feet all round.

'Move on,' the detective said without effect. 'Break it up now. There's nothing to see . . . Now you take it easy. We'll get you out of here and have that eye seen to. You'll need a stitch . . .'

On his feet, he swayed slightly and the faces blurred. Still they waited, though, and watched. Something would happen.

Frank charged into them in a swaying run, the detective following. He broke into the clear then hit congestion again by the Ice Drome and elbowed right and left. 'Let me pass.'

But they were dummies, as blank and uncomprehending as the orchestra of animals miming with stiff movements to music from a hidden loudspeaker, on the left. As lifeless and uncaring as the little man in the glass case outside the Fun House, whose strident mechanical laughter carried on a sudden spring of breeze made the best comment yet on Frank's efforts: 'Hoh, hoh, hoh, hoh, hoh, hoh, hoh.'

Straining, swearing, elbowing, he caught, suddenly, where the twin tracks of the Grand National scenic railway swooped under the roadway to the finishing post, a glimpse of Arny poised on a railing.

A woman's scream cut through the thunder of approaching railcars. The detective caught Frank as he swayed and nearly fell.

Chapter Forty-eight

A man who was kneeling beside him got to his feet after drawing a raincoat up to Arny's throat. He caught Feather's eye and shook his head.

'There's an ambulance on its way,' Feather said. He looked at Frank. 'I thought we had him, then he went over the rail, straight in front of the cars. What a pity. What made him run? Did he tumble to it?'

'Frank . . .'

Arny had opened his eyes. His face was unmarked but its pallor was waxen. Frank got down beside him.

'How do you feel?'

'Fucking terrible.'

'Don't try to talk.'

'Don't now, never shall.'

'There's an ambulance coming. They'll have you fixed up in no time.'

'Cut the crap, lad.' His lips drew back in a snarl of pain and something moved feebly under the coat. Frank found and held his hand. 'Jee-eze . . .'

'Take it easy.'

'I never thought you'd do it, Frank.'

'I didn't, Arny. It wasn't me.'

'Well, how the . . .? Never mind. Won't hang me now, will they? Thankful for small mercies, eh?' His face twisted again and his eyes closed tight as he was drawn back to where there was nothing but his agony, awareness packed to the limits with pain.

'Have I . . . Have I any legs down there?'

'Of course you have.'

Arny shut his eyes again. His lips opened and closed as though his throat was parched. Frank was about to ask for some water for him when Arny opened his eyes and spoke again.

'Listen . . .'

'I'm listening.'

'Tell my father . . .'

'Yes?'

'Tell him . . . Tell him it's all a big con . . . Tell him I've looked over . . . I've seen it, and there's . . . there's nothing there . . . Tell him . . .'

The grip on Frank's hand relaxed. He withdrew it, intending to wipe Arny's forehead. He took out his handkerchief and saw how indistinguishably his blood and Arny's mingled in the bright stain on the linen. Somebody spoke to him. He glanced up without understanding and when he looked back Arny was gone.

Later

Chapter Forty-nine

'And what about you, lad?' Frank's uncle asked. 'What are you going to do?' Knowing without saying that nothing could resume as before.

There had been a funeral of sorts. Aunt Carrie had gone straight upstairs. The day was chilly with rain. A pale flame or two struggled in the living-room grate where Uncle Vernon had just put a match to the laid fire.

'I've had a promising letter from the BBC.'

'Oh?' The magic letters evoked the usual respect.

'The Northern Region Music Department. They've seen some of my arrangements and they'd like to talk to me.'

'Good, good. Music's always been what you really wanted, hasn't it?'

'Yes.'

'We still have the piano.'

'Yes.'

'Nobody plays it now.' Uncle Vernon fidgeted, withdrawn again on the slow irregular pulse of his preoccupation. 'It's worth a lot in money,' he said after a little start, 'if you're doing what you want to do.'

'I've always thought so.'

Again he seemed to go away. But he had seen that the fire was not drawing and in a moment he spread the *Daily Herald* and held it across the opening until the flames roared. He glanced at Frank as he turned and put the paper aside.

'Are you going to reproach yourself over any of this?'

Frank shifted uneasily in his chair.

'I'm afraid you will, because you're that sort.'

'I don't know what I could have done that—'

'You could have turned him in,' Uncle Vernon said. 'Taken him off the street as soon as you found out; so that he couldn't harm anybody else.'

'Do you really think so?'

'I said you could have. I wasn't taken in by all that was said at the inquest. You tried to warn him, didn't you?'

'Yes, I did.'

'What made you do that when you loathed both what he'd done and what he'd become?'

'It was after I knew the old man was dead; when I knew what they'd very likely do to Arny. I couldn't connive in that.'

'It's the law, Frank.'

'It won't always be.'

'You shouldn't take too much on yourself, son. There's a greater judge than any of us.'

'Some of us,' Frank said, 'have to try to be good without God.'

'And a lonely business it must be.'

'He said to tell you,' Frank began. 'At the end, he said to tell you he was sorry. He'd made a mess of things.'

For the first time that morning he felt himself the focus of his uncle's attention.

'It doesn't sound like him.' Frank gestured with his hand. 'I knew him better than you seem to think, Frank, and I don't need white lies for comfort. I'd rather you told me the truth.'

'He wasn't afraid.'

'I've wondered about that. I've wondered whether he was defiant to the last.'

'I wouldn't have called it that,' Frank said.

'I've wondered as well, many and many a time – before all this – I've wondered, why him? Why not you, if anybody? You were the one who was pushed around. He had everything you hadn't.'

Frank did not try to respond.

'He came late, you know, after many prayers. He was the most wonderful gift your aunt and I could have imagined. A child. You can't see then why it won't always be as fine and lovely as that feeling. But soon it takes on its own life. At first that independence, that will, amuse you. You think you still have control. The last word. You give it a loving home. You feed and clothe and educate it. You try to teach it to know right from wrong, good from evil, and how to live a full and decent life. When you've done all that there's nothing left but to pray. And one day you turn round and realise that what you started with – all that was fine and lovely and good – has vanished and left something strange and frightening. You can't understand any of it then.'

Uncle Vernon blinked rapidly a number of times. He stood up. This time it was a signal. Frank followed suit.

'Keep in touch, Frank.' For a moment, as they lifted to Frank's face, Uncle Vernon's eyes seemed to register something outside his preoccupation.

'That girl. With the uncle . . .'

'Rona?'

'Is she all right?'

'She's an absolutely marvellous girl, Uncle.'

'Well, then . . .'

'Of course, it's early days yet . . .'

'But you can work on that?'

'Yes.'

'Good. I'm very pleased. Very pleased. Let us know how you fare.'

Us . . . 'I ought to say goodbye to Aunt Carrie.'

His uncle shook his head. 'She won't come down now. Try to bear with her, Frank. She hasn't a broad view. Perhaps one day she'll . . . If you can bring yourself to it then, well . . . Just now she knows nothing bar one thing: she's lost her only child.'

There seemed to be something in the corner of Uncle Vernon's eye. He felt for it, then examined the end of his finger.

159

Chapter Fifty

A cold thin rain was falling as Frank went out. He noticed again, as he had noticed scores of times before, how it glazed and darkened to the colour of plums the gable-end brickwork of the house opposite.

As he paused to latch the gate he sensed rather than saw the movement of a lace curtain at an upstairs window of the house he had just left. Resisting the impulse to look up, he turned and walked away along the street, squaring his shoulders and lifting his bare head. Perhaps one day, he was thinking, he would know for certain whether he had been right or wrong, strong or weak. Certain in his own mind and no one else's. One thing he already knew for sure was that he would need help along the way and he thought he knew now where to find that. But the final coming to terms would be for him alone. For he was Frank and no one else and that was how it should be.

THE END